HER RETURN
TO KING'S BED

—

MAUREEN CHILD

D0004048

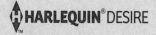
HARLEQUIN® DESIRE

Recycling programs
for this product may
not exist in your area.

ISBN-13: 978-0-373-73282-1

HER RETURN TO KING'S BED

Printed in U.S.A.

"What Exactly Is It That You Want From Me, Rico?"

"I want *you*," Rico said flatly.

The ice inside Teresa melted in a flash. "You what?"

"I want you here. In my bed."

"You do?"

"For one month," he qualified, splintering her fantasies. "You're lucky I'm not demanding the *five years* that you were gone. You will stay here for one month. You will share my bed like a good wife."

"You're *not* going to blackmail me into sex."

"Of course not. But we will sleep in the same bed. And when we *do* have sex again, Teresa, it will be your idea. You remember how good it was between us...."

Oh, she really did.

"Blackmail isn't necessary for what lies between us."

He was right, God help her.

* * *

Her Return to King's Bed
is part of the Kings of California series:

Money and power can get the King men
anything...but love.

* * *

If you're on Twitter,
tell us what you think of Harlequin Desire!
#harlequindesire

Dear Reader,

Sometimes in a book, you meet a character who just sticks with you. That happened to me when I was writing a book called *Marrying for King's Millions*. While writing about Travis King and Julie, the woman who married him, I met Rico King. Travis's cousin Rico was tall, dark, handsome and very mysterious.

I knew Rico would have his own book... He is a King, after all. But his heroine had to be just right, so I waited until Teresa Coretti showed up in my daydreams and I knew she was perfect for Rico.

In the King family, loyalty is everything. So when Rico is convinced that Teresa betrayed him—right after their wedding—he's determined to make her pay. But having Teresa Coretti King back in his life just may mean that Rico is the one who will pay.

I really hope you enjoy this book. I loved writing it and so many of you have written asking for Rico's story that I truly hope you're pleased with it!

Visit me on Facebook, on Twitter or at my website, www.maureenchild.com.

And as always, thanks so much for your continuing support!

Happy reading,

Maureen

Books by Maureen Child

Harlequin Desire

Silhouette Desire

Other titles by this author
available in ebook format.

MAUREEN CHILD

writes for Harlequin Desire and can't imagine a better job. Being able to indulge your love for romance as well as being able to spin stories just the way you want them told is, in a word, perfect.

A seven-time finalist for the prestigious Romance Writers of America RITA® Award, Maureen is the author of more than one hundred romance novels. Her books regularly appear on the bestseller lists and have won several awards, including a Prism, a National Readers' Choice Award, a Colorado Romance Writers Award of Excellence and a Golden Quill.

Maureen believes that laughter goes hand in hand with love, so her stories are always filled with humor. The many letters she receives assures her that her readers love to laugh as much as she does.

Maureen Child is a native Californian, but has recently moved to the mountains of Utah. She loves a new adventure, though the thought of having to deal with snow for the first time is a little intimidating.

To my husband, the man who is always there when I need him and who still makes me laugh every day. I love you.

One

"A jewel thief?" Rico King demanded of his chief of security. "Here in the hotel?"

Franklin Hicks scowled. The man was late thirties, stood six foot five and boasted a shaved head and sharp blue eyes. "Only explanation. The guest in bungalow six—Serenity James—reported that some of her diamonds are missing. I've already interviewed the maid and room service."

Bungalow six. Rico could have pulled up the map of the hotel on his computer, but there was no need. He knew every inch of his place. He knew that the bungalows were set apart from the main hotel—for privacy, since a lot of his clientele insisted on seclusion. People like Serenity James, an up-and-coming Hollywood darling who, in spite of her name, lived life on the edge.

The actress might claim to want to avoid photographers and nosy guests, but according to security, there were men streaming in and out of her bungalow at all hours. Any one of them could have made off with the diamonds. He hoped it would be that easy.

"What about Ms. James's 'guests'?" Rico looked up at the other man. "Did you talk to them, as well?"

Snorting, Franklin admitted, "We're still running them all to ground, but I don't think it was one of them, boss. If those diamonds were taken by one of her 'guests,' they'd have helped themselves to more than just the one necklace. Whoever took the diamonds was picky about it. Took the stones that would be easiest to pry out of their settings and sell. Smells like a professional job to me. Besides, you have to remember we've had two more reports of stolen property in the last few days. Gotta be a pro."

"Not good news," Rico mused.

His hotel, the Tesoro Castle, had only been open for a little more than six months. It was new, fresh and exclusive and had quickly become the hot spot for celebrities and the überwealthy who were looking for a private getaway spot. Tesoro Island sat in the middle of the Caribbean, but it was privately owned. No one landed here—private yacht or cruise ship—without permission of the owner, Walter Stanford.

Which meant that those seeking privacy had nothing to fear from paparazzi, except for the occasional overachiever who used telephoto lenses from a boat anchored far offshore.

Tesoro was lush and secluded, and the Castle was like Disneyland for adults: there were infinity pools, the best spas in the world and sweeping ocean views from every room. The hotel had deliberately been built small, to keep it a select destination. There were only a hundred and fifty rooms, not counting the private bungalows scattered across the grounds. The interiors were opulent, service was impeccable and the island itself carried an air of dreamy seduction. For those who could afford it, Tesoro promised a world of languid pleasures for all of the senses.

And damned if Rico was going to allow his hotel's reputation to be stained. If there was a professional thief operating in his place, then that thief would be found.

"Security cameras?" Rico demanded.

"Nothing." Franklin scowled as if the word tasted bitter. "Another reason to go with the professional thief theory. Whoever it was, they knew how to bypass the cameras."

Perfect.

"Set up a meeting with your men. I want eyes and ears everywhere. If you need to hire more security," Rico said, "call my cousin Griffin. King Security can have more men here tomorrow if we need them."

Franklin bristled. He'd once worked for Griffin King and his twin, Garrett, and had decided to leave in favor of being chief of security here on the island. He clearly didn't care for the suggestion that there might be something he couldn't handle. "I won't need more men. The team I've got is the best in the world. Now that I know we're looking for a pro, we'll find him."

Rico nodded. He understood pride and he knew that Franklin's had been pricked. He was in charge and having a professional thief on the grounds was a direct slap in the face. But pride notwithstanding, if Rico decided they needed more help, Franklin would get extra men whether he liked it or not.

This hotel had been Rico's dream. Built to his exact

specifications by King Construction, the Tesoro Castle was the epitome of luxury hotels. He'd been working toward this project for all of his adult life. He owned several hotels and each in its own way was spectacular. But this place on Tesoro was his crowning achievement. He'd do whatever he had to do to protect his name and his investment.

Shaking his head in irritation, Rico turned and stared out his office window at the view spread out below him. The island of Tesoro, Spanish for "treasure," was aptly named.

Miles of unspoiled beaches, aquamarine ocean, thick jungles with amazing waterfalls hidden away in the stands of trees. Sunshine every damn day and unlike most of the Caribbean, the trade winds blew across Tesoro almost constantly, keeping the heat—and flying insects—at bay.

Rico had spent months with Walter Stanford, negotiating for his own slice of the old man's paradise. Hell, he'd even had some of his cousins come in and talk to the older man for him. Of course, Rico mused, that had worked out for Sean King, since he'd married Walter's granddaughter Melinda.

After the negotiations, the months spent building this place and the time and expense of furnishing and staffing this hotel to get it just right…irritation blossomed into quietly restrained fury. No one was going to ruin this place.

His guests came to Tesoro looking for beauty, privacy and security and he would see that they got it.

Just the thought of jewel thieves on the island had him gritting his teeth and flexing his hands into fists that had no one to punch. He supposed it was only natural that thieves would find their way here to Tesoro, where the rich flocked in droves. Just as it was natural that when he found whoever was behind this, he'd see them locked away for decades.

But a professional thief risked a lot to make a play on Tesoro. The island was too small. Too difficult to get to and to leave from. And since no ships had left the harbor in days, whoever the thief was, he was still on the island and he still had the stolen property on him.

Jewel thieves.

Suddenly, those two words began to echo over and over again in his mind as warning bells started clanging inside his head. Even then, though, Rico assured himself that the little voice inside his head had to be wrong.

No way would she risk that.

Not even *she* would have the nerve to chance facing him again.

But what if she had?

"Boss?"

"What?" Rico glanced over his shoulder at Franklin.

"You want me to contact Interpol about this?"

The international police force with hundreds of member countries didn't make arrests or have its own jail, but it could and did provide much-needed data on suspected thieves, killers and just about any crime imaginable.

"No," he said, ignoring the look of surprise on his head of security's face. Instead, he turned back to look out the window over the playground he'd built for the rich and famous. Rico's brain was racing with possibilities and his adrenaline surged at the idea that he just might be at the threshold of the revenge he'd waited five years to take.

No chance in hell he'd bring Interpol into this before he knew whether or not his gut instinct was right or not.

"We'll handle it on island," he said, never taking his gaze from the horizon, where the sunlight glinted off the water in bright shards. "Once we've got the thief, we'll decide what to do then."

"Your call," Franklin said, then he left, closing the office door behind him.

"Yeah, it is," Rico told himself aloud. And if this jewel thief turned out to be the woman who'd stolen from him once before…Interpol would be lucky if there was anything left of her to hand over.

"Papa, please. Leave now before it's too late." Teresa Coretti glanced from her father to the closed door of his suite and back again.

She was so anxious just being here on Tesoro, even her nerves had nerves. But she'd had to come. The moment she'd realized where her father and brother had gone on their supposed vacation, Teresa had had no choice.

"How can I leave?" her father asked with an exaggerated shrug and a smile. "I've not finished my holiday."

Holiday.

If only.

If Nick Coretti was really taking a sabbatical from his avocation, no one at the Tesoro Castle would have lost any of their possessions. No, her father could call this a holiday if he wanted to, but the truth was he was working. As he always was.

Dominick was a shorter, older, Italian version of George Clooney. His tan was permanent, and his sharp brown eyes missed nothing. His black hair was gray-streaked, but that only seemed to give him an air of distinction. He was polished and always a gentleman. He had been a faithful husband until Teresa's mother's death ten years ago.

Since then, he had used his considerable charm to smooth his way into high society, where, he said, "the pickings are always worth the effort." He loved women; women loved him. And he was the best jewel thief in the world—not counting Teresa's brothers, Gianni and Paulo.

Her father was always on the lookout for his next job. She should have known that he would never have been able to resist the allure of Tesoro. For him, it was the mother lode.

The problem was, this fabulous hotel belonged to Rico King and that was really not a good thing.

It had been five years since she'd seen Rico and just thinking his name sent a ripple of heat along her spine. Like it was yesterday, she could see those blue eyes of his as he stared down at her. She could almost taste his mouth on hers and hardly a night went by that she didn't dream of his hands sliding across her skin.

She'd spent so much time trying to get Rico out of her mind as well as her life—and here she was. On *his* turf.

Warily, she turned her head for a quick look outside to the terrace, as if half expecting to see Rico standing there. Glaring at her.

But the elegantly furnished deck was empty save for the glass-topped table, the chairs and matching chaise and a silver bucket holding her father's favorite brand of champagne. Which, she thought, brought her right back to the problem at hand.

"Papa," she started, "I asked you to stay away from Rico King, remember?"

Nick flicked an imaginary piece of lint from the elegantly tailored suit jacket he wore, then smoothed one hand along the side of his perfectly styled hair. "Of course I remember, my angel. And as promised," he continued, wagging a finger at her, "I have refused all temptation to relieve Mr. King of his valuables."

Teresa sighed. "That's not what I meant, Papa. Tesoro is Rico's. Being here, stealing from his guests, you might as well be lifting *his* wallet. You're tempting fate, Papa. Rico is not exactly an understanding man."

"Ah, Teresa," Nick said, carrying his crystal flute to the terrace where he refilled his glass and took a sip before continuing. "You were always too nervous. Too..." He paused, tipped his head back and tried to come up with the right word. Finally, he added sadly, *"Honest."*

A wry smile curved Teresa's mouth. Where else but in her family would honesty be considered a fatal flaw? She'd lived on the fringes of the law since she was a child. Before she was five, she could identify a plainclothes police officer as well as a possible mark with alacrity. While other children played with dolls, Teresa learned to pick locks. When her girlfriends were taking driver's education, Teresa studied with her uncle Antonio, the master safecracker.

She loved her family, but she'd never been comfortable with stealing for a living. At eighteen, she had broken it to her father that she had gone on her last job. Instead, she became the first Coretti in memory to go to school and be legally, gainfully employed.

Her father still considered it a tragic waste of her talents.

While her mind raced, she watched her father settle on the chaise and stare off at the resort spread below.

Rico had built something amazing here, she thought, but that didn't surprise her. He was a man who never settled for less than the best, no matter the circumstances. She'd learned that when she first met him so long ago in Cancún.

At his hotel, Castello de King—King's Castle—Teresa had been one of the innumerable chefs in the immense hotel kitchens. In her first real job after culinary school, she was excited simply to be a part of the hustle that took place in that amazing kitchen. Teresa had believed that working in that hotel was the best thing that had ever happened to her—until she met Rico himself.

She'd worked late one night and before heading to her apartment, Teresa had treated herself to a little relaxation. She'd carried a glass of wine out to one of the beach lounge chairs and sat to enjoy the night, the moon on the water and the lovely sensation of being absolutely *alone*.

Then *he* had appeared, walking along the water's edge, moonlight shining on his dark hair and making the white shirt he wore seem to glow. He'd worn tan slacks and his bare feet had kicked through the water with every step. She couldn't seem to look away from him. He was tall and dark and as he came closer, she realized he was *gorgeous*. He was also her employer. Rico King, playboy, gazillionaire, hotelier and at the moment, as alone as she.

In an instant, her mind replayed that scene.

He glanced up as if sensing her gaze on him and when he saw her, he smiled and headed for her. "I thought I was alone on the beach."

"So did I," she managed to say.

"Shall we be alone together?"

Teresa still remembered that faintest hint of an accent coloring his words. His eyes were a piercing blue, his hair as black as the night and his smile was temptation personified. She couldn't have said no to him even if she had tried—which she hadn't. Rico had sat on the sand beside her and they'd shared her glass of wine and spent the next couple of hours talking.

Teresa came out of the memory and mentally warned herself to stop reliving the past. To stop indulging in thoughts of him and what might have been. She was here on Tesoro—in Rico's hotel—for one reason only: to get her family out of there before Rico discovered them. If only her father had listened to her. But Nick Coretti was a force of nature and when the prize was rich, no risk was too much.

Rico *would* find them. Teresa knew that man too well to think that he would allow jewel thieves to operate freely in his place. It was only a matter of time. Which meant that she had to get the Coretti family off Tesoro. Fast.

Teresa followed her father to the terrace. The sunlight was bright, the sky a brilliant blue and a soft breeze carried the scent of tropical flowers as it lifted her hair off her neck.

"Papa, you don't know Rico like I do. He *will* catch you."

Her father snorted, then shook his head and chuckled. "*Bellissima,* no Coretti has *ever* been caught. We are too good at what we do."

True, she thought, but the Corettis had never come up against an adversary like Rico before, either. Yes, various police forces from several countries had tried and failed to pin a crime on the Corettis. But their interest in the family of thieves had been purely professional.

For Rico, this would be personal.

"Papa, you have to trust me on this." She laid one hand on his arm. "Please, let's get off the island while we still can."

He clucked his tongue at her. "You have made far too much of this man you once cared for. Always you believe he is searching for you. Searching for *us*."

"He did search for me, remember?"

Nick waved that away. "You pricked his pride when you left him, my darling. It is understandable. No man would care for losing such a lovely woman from his life. But it's now five years. I believe it's time you stop worrying about this man."

Five years or five minutes. Rico was the kind of man who *never* left a woman's thoughts.

Besides, her father didn't know everything that had happened between her and Rico. Some things she hadn't been able to share, not even with her family.

Watching her father now, looking like the lord of the manor as he stared out over the luxurious view spread below him, she thought that under any other circumstances, he and Rico might have been friends. They were two of the most stubborn, willful men she had ever known.

And realizing that meant she had to admit she was fighting a losing battle. Dominick Coretti would never leave a job half-finished. And now that he had begun to infiltrate the guests at the Castle, he wouldn't leave until he was good and ready.

Which made him a sitting duck for Rico. Every hotelier in the world knew the Corettis. They weren't invisible. They were simply so good at what they did, there was never any evidence against them. They were high profile, wealthy and they didn't hide in out-of-the-way spots. Nick Coretti, like all of those who came before him, believed in living his life to the fullest. The fact that he did it with other people's money didn't change anything.

Ordinarily Teresa might have worried that coming here herself would give up the game because Rico would notice her. But her family was here. In plain sight. And now diamonds were missing. Rico would put the two together.

Her father stood, poured more champagne and stepped to the wrought-iron lace of the balcony railing. He might have been enjoying the view, but Teresa knew him well enough to know that he was looking not at the resort, but at its guests. He would be scoping them out, looking for his next target—assuming he hadn't already chosen one.

For all his charm, Dominick wasn't a man to be crossed. As head of the Coretti family, he might as well have been a general ordering his troops around. When he made a plan, that was it. The rest of the family fell in line.

Except for Teresa. As a kid, she'd been intrigued by the Coretti family legacy. As a teenager, she'd begun wishing that they could stay put in their house outside Naples. That she could *belong,* instead of traipsing all over Europe. They never stayed in one place more than a month and only came back to their home base occasionally, so it was impossible to make friends. Teresa and her brothers had been homeschooled and along with the usual—history, math and such—had taken classes on lock picking, safecracking and forgery. By the time the Coretti children were adults, they were each prepared to carry on the family dynasty.

That was when Teresa had taken her stand. Her father had raged and argued, her mother had wept and her brothers hadn't really believed she would do it. But in the end, Teresa had become the one Coretti in generations who *hadn't* joined the family business. Which made her a puzzle to her brothers and an irritation to her father.

"You're making too much of this, Teresa," he chided now with a sad shake of his head. "This is no different from any other job, and when we have finished, we will be gone. With no one the wiser."

"You're wrong, Papa," she argued again. "You don't know Rico as I do. He's a dangerous man."

Dangerous to *her,* anyway.

That got Nick's attention. "Did this man harm you in some way? If he did—"

"No." She interrupted him quickly. The problem, she thought, was that the Coretti family had a history with Rico that her father knew nothing about. And now wasn't the time to tell the story. "He didn't hurt me. But Papa, he won't allow thieves to operate in his place. He'll find you and when he does…"

"What can he do?" Nick laughed a little and sipped at his champagne. "He will have no proof of anything. You should know better, Teresa. The Coretti family is not so easy to catch."

"Obviously it is not as difficult as you might wish." A deep, familiar voice spoke up from directly behind her.

Teresa went absolutely still.

She would know that voice anywhere.

With a weird mixture of dread and anticipation, she slowly turned and looked into the eyes of Rico King.

Two

"What's the meaning of this?" the older man in the room demanded, striding in from the terrace to face Rico. "Who are you? What are you doing in my suite?"

"Papa," Teresa said, rising from her chair, "this is Rico King."

"Ah," Nick mused with a half smile. "Our host. Still, this doesn't give you the right to intrude uninvited."

Rico steamed silently and hated the fact that he had to *force* his gaze away from Teresa's to meet her father's. The glint in the other man's eyes told Rico the older Coretti had known exactly who Rico was. This was all part of the game. "The fact that you're a thief on my property gives me all of the rights I need."

"Thief?" The older man bristled and puffed up until his chest was so full of air, Rico wouldn't have been surprised to see him lift off the floor and float about the room.

"Papa, please." Teresa stepped in between the two men like a referee interrupting a prizefight. Facing Rico, she said, "We'll leave. Right away."

"You're not going anywhere," he told her and felt that bubble of righteous anger fuel him again.

Five years, he told himself. Five long years wondering where the hell she was. If she was dead or injured. If she was laughing at him from some other man's bed. No. She wasn't leaving. Not until he was good and ready for her to be gone. And at the moment, he didn't know just when that might be.

She went pale and her brown eyes shone with too many banked emotions to identify. If he had cared to try. Which he didn't, he assured himself. Instead, Rico dismissed her and focused his gaze on the other man in the room.

Dominick Coretti was stylish, confident and even now Rico could see the gleam of exhilaration in his eyes. He was already trying to think of a way out. A way to salvage a situation that had turned on him unexpectedly. Well, there was no way out for him—unless he did exactly as Rico wanted.

"I am insulted that you would think me a thief," Nick began, clearly sticking to his routine of outraged guest. "And I will not stay where I am clearly unwelcome. My family and I will book passage off the island by this evening."

"Your family will not be allowed to leave until the jewelry you've taken has been returned."

"I beg your pardon—"

"There is no pardon here," Rico told him flatly. Oh, he had to hand it to the man. He was pulling off the insulted-guest routine so well that if Rico hadn't been sure of his facts, he might have believed him. Problem was, there was no doubt in Rico's mind just who the Coretti family really was.

"Once the jewelry is returned," he said with a knowing smile, "you and your son can leave. My *wife* will remain with me."

"Wife?" Nick echoed.

"Wife?" Teresa yelped.

Finally, Rico looked to her again and was pleased to see stunned shock on her beautiful features. Her eyes were wide, her mouth open and color had rushed in to fill her pale, honey-toned cheeks.

"That's crazy."

"It's true."

"You said nothing to me of marrying this man," her father accused.

"It wasn't important," she argued without even glancing at the other man.

Those three words slapped at Rico and only served to fan the flames of his anger. *Not important.* Their marriage. Her running out on him. Her family stealing what was his. *Not important.* Anger was rife inside him and he struggled to keep his tone and his expression from revealing his feelings. "That's not what you said at the time."

"How is it I was not told of this marriage?" The accusatory tone in her father's voice singed the air.

"Papa—"

Rico didn't believe the other man's outrage for a second. He knew all about the Corettis. He'd done his research over the last several years. And though the private investigators he'd hired hadn't been able to locate Teresa, they'd come up with quite a bit of very interesting information. Enough to see the whole damn family locked away, if he wished.

So, no, he didn't believe Nick's performance. He knew that thieving had been a way of life for the family for generations. Lying was their stock in trade.

"I'm not playing this game," he said simply, quietly.

"Game?"

He glanced at the older man, then shifted his gaze back to the woman who haunted him. "As I said, return the jewelry you stole and you and your son can leave the island. Teresa will stay here. With *me,* until you bring me the gold dagger that was taken from me five years ago."

"You cannot hold my daughter here against her will," Nick said, the steel in his voice telling Rico this was a man accustomed to being obeyed.

"It's that," Rico said, staring at the other man now, "or I go to Interpol."

Nick waved that threat away with a negligent, well-manicured hand. "Interpol doesn't worry me."

"Once I hand over the information I have gathered on your family over the years, I think you'll feel differently."

Dark brown eyes narrowed. "What information?"

"Enough to end you," Rico promised, ignoring Teresa's soft gasp.

"Impossible," Nick blustered, but concern glinted in his eyes. "There has never been evidence found against my family."

"Until now." Rico gave him a smile. "Private investigators can go where the police can't. And if the law should receive this information from an anonymous source…"

Nick Coretti—or Candello, as he was registered here—looked as if he'd been cornered. And he had.

Now the years of hiring the best private investigators in the world and collecting data and evidence were finally paying off—just as he'd known it would one day. Rico had been methodical as only a King could be when faced with an enemy. Add to that heritage the Latin blood that swam in his veins and revenge tasted sweeter than he had even imagined.

"Your sons are not always as careful as their father," he said, watching suspicion and then a cautious wariness shine in Dominick Coretti's eyes.

"You're bluffing."

Rico smiled slightly and, without taking his gaze from Nick's, said, "Teresa, tell your father I don't bluff."

"He doesn't, Papa," she whispered and the sound seemed to echo in the plush suite. "If he says he has evidence, he does."

A frown crossed Nick's face then and Rico knew he had the man's attention.

"What is it you want?"

"I've already told you. I want what your family stole from me five years ago."

Nick shot a look at his daughter. "I think you stole something from me, as well."

He hadn't *stolen* Teresa, Rico thought. He'd let his heart rule his head for the first and last time in his life. And just look where that had gotten him.

"Fine, then," he said. "Call it an exchange. You return my property and I will return yours."

He knew he was being insulting and he just didn't give a royal damn.

"Property?" Teresa hissed the word as her back went poker straight and her shoulders squared as if for battle.

She lifted her chin and looked up at Rico. "I'm no one's property. Least of all *yours*."

He inclined his head in a nod. "Don't bother being offended. I'm not interested in keeping you."

She reacted as if she'd been slapped.

Rico ignored her. "You can go as soon as I have the Aztec dagger back in my possession."

Not only had Teresa used him and then vanished, she'd done her disappearing act right after the centuries-old dagger had gone missing from Rico's collection. He knew, thanks to information his P.I.s had gathered, that Teresa's brother had stolen it from him. And he wanted that dagger. It was a ceremonial dagger, used in the Aztecs' religious sacrifices, that Rico's great-great-however-many-greats-grandfather had found in an archaeological dig more than two hundred years ago. Not only was it ancient and a piece of history—it had been handed down in his father's family for longer than anyone could remember—and Rico would have it returned.

Once he had that—and his personal revenge on Teresa—he could be done with her and the past.

As if Nick wasn't in the room with them, Teresa took a single step closer to him before stopping herself. Staring up into his eyes, she said, "I got a divorce five years ago. I hired an attorney in Cancún and he filed the papers. He sent me the final decree."

"It was a fake," he said sharply.

Rage escalated as he remembered her attorney, a good friend of Rico's, coming to him, telling him about Teresa's divorce plans. Because that attorney had owed Rico, he'd given his allegiance to him rather than his client. Together, they'd faked a divorce decree and let her believe the marriage had been dissolved. Of course, he had tried to use the address she gave the lawyer to find her. But she had disappeared again, losing herself somewhere in Europe.

There had been a few times over the last five years that Rico had regretted his decision. But at the time, he'd been too tormented by the way she'd left. Too furious at the way she'd used him only to vanish, to let her go. And still too…enamored of her to allow that disappearance to be final.

Now he was glad he'd done it. For the satisfaction of seeing her shock, if for nothing else. She had thought herself in charge. Assumed that she had left him behind in her tangle of lies.

Even now, he knew she was wondering how he'd found her here. How he'd managed to pluck her from the hundreds of guests currently staying at the Castle.

It hadn't been hard.

As owner of the hotel, he had access to the guest registry and finding Teresa had been surprisingly easy. She'd signed in under the name Teresa Cucinare—Italian for "cook." Once he suspected her of the thievery, he had zeroed in on her, then confirmed his suspicions with a quick talk with the front desk.

When his employee had described Teresa Cucinare as drop-dead gorgeous with wide brown eyes and a dimple in her right cheek, Rico knew he had her.

Five years, three months and ten days.

Not that Rico was counting or anything. But he knew down to the damn minute when this woman—*his* woman—had disappeared.

He'd spent a lot of time thinking about what he would say to her. What he would do when he finally found her. And now here she was and all he could do was stare at her.

He finally allowed himself the time to simply drink her in. From the top of her head down her incredibly lush and curvy body to the tips of her red-painted toes, displayed so nicely in her high-heeled sandals.

Hunger roared to life inside him and smothered even the rage and frustration that had been Rico's constant companions these last five years. She'd married him. Used him. And then left him looking like a damn fool. There was no forgiveness for that, Rico told himself.

But damn, she looked even better now than she had when they were together. Clearly, the last five years hadn't been difficult ones for Teresa Coretti.

Coretti.

When he'd married her, he'd had no idea that her last name was infamous throughout Europe. He'd discovered that much later, after she had gone. He'd been able to follow her trail as far as Italy, but after that, it was as if she'd gone up in a puff of smoke. She was as adept at protecting herself as the rest of her family was. The police had never been able to pin a crime on the Corettis and Rico hadn't been able to find her, no matter how many P.I.s he'd hired in so many different countries he'd lost count.

But all of that was over now. He had her. Here. At his place. And damned if she'd get away from him again.

"Rico—"

Her voice was low, breathless, sexy enough to jolt through him like a bolt of lightning. Damn, Rico hated to admit—even to himself—that he was still affected by her. Five years and he still wanted her more than his next breath.

But this time that want, that need, would be assuaged on *his* terms.

"Been a long time," he finally said, keeping his gaze fixed with hers.

"I know—"

"What amazes me—" he spoke quickly, interrupting whatever she might have said "—is that you had the guts to show up here."

"If you'll let me explain…"

"Why? So you can spout whatever lies you've rehearsed for this occasion?" He shook his head. "I don't think so."

"Now, I think we can all discuss this in a civilized manner."

Rico's gaze darted to Teresa's father. Dominick Coretti. Head of a family of thieves and no doubt the man who had taught his daughter her precarious sense of honor. Studying him, Rico had to give the man credit. Caught red-handed, Nick Coretti looked unflappable. As if nothing more important had happened than his champagne had gone flat. This despite the fact that everyone in the room *knew* that he'd been outmaneuvered.

"Civilized?" Rico repeated. "Is it civilized to steal from others? Is it civilized to use your daughter to keep a man busy so that you can steal from him?"

Nick's eyes narrowed. "I don't use my children."

"Just train them, do you?" Rico sneered.

"That's enough." Teresa took a breath and then, deliberately turning her back on Rico, she faced her father. "Papa, will you excuse us?"

The older man looked from his daughter to Rico and back again. "Are you certain, Teresa?"

"I'll be fine," she assured him. "Please."

"Very well." Nick tugged at the lapels of his suit, lifted his chin and met Rico's gaze. "I will not be far."

"That would be best," Rico told him. "And I would advise that you not consider trying to leave the island."

Nick stiffened, clearly insulted. "I would not slink away like a coward, leaving my daughter behind."

Rico wasn't so sure, but since he was anxious to get the man out of the room, he didn't say so aloud. Instead, he waited until Nick had left the suite before saying to Teresa, "The harbor's closed. He won't get out."

"He wouldn't leave me," she said stiffly.

"Honor among thieves, you mean?" Rico snorted a laugh. "Hard to believe coming from the woman who used me just long enough for her family to steal what was mine."

"I didn't—" She stopped, shook her head and muttered something he couldn't catch before she looked up at him. "What did you mean when you said we're not divorced?"

"Just that. The decree your lawyer sent you was a forgery."

She huffed out a breath and folded her arms across her chest. "A forgery." Swinging her long fall of hair back behind her shoulder, she fired a glare at him. "And I'm guessing that was your idea."

"It was."

She sucked in a gulp of air. "You've got a lot of nerve calling my family cheats and liars. You're no better."

"That's where you're wrong," he told her, moving in closer, pleased when she scurried back a step or two. "I never stole from you. I never lied to you. I didn't *use* you."

"Maybe not," she countered, "but you tricked me. You let me believe we were finished. And why? So you could find me and what, keep me locked in a dungeon here on the island?"

He gave her a small smile. "Sadly, I have no dungeon here at the hotel. But I'm sure I can come up with something appropriate."

"You can't be serious." Teresa gave a quick look to either side of her, as if expecting help to come riding to her rescue. But there was nothing. They were still alone in the luxury suite and the tension simmering between them grew thicker by the moment.

"I've never been more serious." He leaned in close to her ear and whispered, "You're still my wife."

He'd waited for this moment. To have her in front of him, telling him to his face that their marriage had been nothing but a lie. That it had been a ruse to allow her family access so they could steal from him.

And now that the moment was here? It was every bit as sweet as he'd dreamed it would be.

She turned her head slightly and glared at him. "You know as well as I that you can't keep me prisoner, Rico."

He shrugged and tucked his hands into the pockets of his black jeans. As his gaze locked with hers, he said, "I won't have to. You'll stay with me of your own accord."

"Why would I do that?"

"I've already told you and your father that I have enough evidence to put the Coretti family in jail for centuries."

"You would do that just to get even with me?"

"Don't doubt it for a moment," he said tightly. "You would be surprised what I might do to someone who deliberately used me. Cheated me."

"I didn't cheat you," she started. "When I found out my brother had—"

"I'm not interested in your explanations," Rico spoke up, cutting her off as he moved in close enough to lay both hands on her shoulders. The feel of her again after all this time was almost too much for him. He steeled himself against his body's instinctive reaction to being with her and focused instead on that still-hot ball of rage in the pit of his stomach. "The time to explain was five years ago, Teresa."

She flinched and he knew his words had been a direct hit. Oddly, that knowledge didn't give him as much pleasure as it should have. "All I want from your family now is what's rightfully mine."

Her eyes widened and as if he could read her thoughts, he shook his head. "No, Teresa. I'm not talking about you. I'm talking about the Aztec dagger your brother took from me. I want it back. And until I get it, you're not going anywhere."

Three

Teresa could have sworn she actually *felt* a lock tumble on the box Rico had trapped her in. He was right. No matter what he wanted or asked or demanded of her, she'd give it, because she couldn't risk her family going to prison.

She felt more vulnerable with Rico now than she had on the night she'd first met the staggeringly sexy man on a deserted Mexican beach. And back then, one look at Rico and her knees had gone weak. Now, though, she couldn't risk showing any weakness at all. The man in front of her might still be her husband—but he was a stranger.

She'd tried to keep up with him, of course. She hadn't been able to rid her mind or heart of his memory, so she'd fed the need to see him by reading tabloids and looking him up on Google. And though it had chewed at her heart to see him squiring some beautiful model or actress around, it had also met the need she had to see his face. He hadn't exactly lived the life of a monk since the last time she'd been with him. But she couldn't hold that against him, could she, since they were divorced.

Or so she'd thought.

"I can't believe we're still married."

His mouth curved into a brief, sardonic smile. "Believe it, Teresa."

She shook her head. "But I paid the attorney. He sent me the final decree."

"Esteban came to me when you hired him," Rico told her. "He owed me a debt."

"And you used me as his payment?"

"You can actually accuse *me* of using *you?*" There was no smile now, only fire flashing in his blue eyes as if the anger churning inside was manifesting into actual flames. "I think we both know the real truth."

She couldn't blame him for believing what he did, but it just wasn't accurate. "I didn't use you, Rico. I wouldn't."

"I would find that easier to believe if you hadn't vanished—along with a valuable antique."

She pushed one hand through her hair, fingers tangling in the thick, black mass. Even now, she could kick her brother Gianni. Five years ago, she'd specifically asked her family to leave Rico alone, but Gianni hadn't been able to help himself. Instead, he'd taken the gold Aztec dagger that Rico prized above everything else. And in doing that, Teresa's brother had made Teresa's decision for her.

"I didn't know the dagger had been stolen until you told me that last morning."

"And I should believe you?"

She sighed. "Believe me or don't."

"Your family took it."

"One of my brothers, yes." God, she was shaking. Seeing him again was so hard. Harder than she would have thought. Seeing him look at her with an angry distance in his eyes was even more difficult.

There had been a time when his eyes shone with passion and something more. Five years ago, she had been swept into a romance so wildly unexpected it had almost been a fairy tale.

And it had all ended with a shattering crash. Much like Cinderella finding herself facing midnight—unwilling to see the magic end.

"I can't believe we're still married. Or that you would go to so much trouble just to punish me."

"You should have known that I wouldn't let you go," he told her.

"I suppose I should have." Teresa looked into his eyes again, hoping to see…what? Love? Passion? Once, she'd seen everything she had ever dreamed of in his eyes. But those days were gone and she had no one to blame but herself. She never should have allowed herself to fall in love with him. And when she did, she never should have kept her identity a secret. Never should have run without at least *trying* to explain. But rewriting the past was a futile mental exercise. Nothing would change what had happened. Nothing would bring back the magic she had once found in Rico's eyes. Because all she read in those blue depths now was a cool detachment that tore at her even as it forced her to adopt a defensive posture.

"What was the point of holding on, Rico? I would

have thought you'd be happy to let me go after the way things ended."

"You took what was mine," he said simply, his features as stony and aloof as an exquisitely carved statue.

For one heart-stopping second, Teresa thought he might have been talking about *her*. That he had considered her important enough to him that he'd purposely kept them legally tied together. Then, as she continued to stare into blue eyes that refused to warm, she admitted the truth to herself. His holding on to her had nothing to do with *her*—it was all about the dagger that Gianni had stolen.

She closed her eyes briefly and wished herself anywhere but here. When she opened her eyes again, though, she was still looking at Rico, still feeling his icy stare dig right through her.

"I didn't know my brother was going to steal the dagger."

He laughed. "You think I believe you?"

"Probably not," she admitted. "But I wanted you to know that."

"Five years later, you decide to try honesty." He shrugged her statement off. "You and your family. Very versatile. You'll even make a wild attempt at the truth if you think it will serve better than a lie."

"This isn't about my family," she argued. "This is about me. And I'm trying to tell you the truth of what happened."

"*Thank you*," he said, sarcasm dripping from the words. "Now I know. It changes nothing." Rico moved past her, walking to the terrace that overlooked the hotel he'd built and the surrounding grounds.

When she followed him, he didn't even look at her

when she spoke. "How long do you plan on keeping me here?"

"Until your thieving family returns my property."

She flushed and was grateful he hadn't seen it. Hard to argue with the truth, no matter how much she'd like to. "This is only about the dagger then?"

"Oh," he said, turning to face her. "It is about much more than that."

The warm, soft trade winds blew across the terrace, ruffling Rico's collar-length black hair. His eyes were shuttered, emotion carefully hidden beneath a veneer of contempt.

She shivered a little at the ice in his gaze and remembered a time when his eyes had held nothing but heat when he looked at her. A time when the two of them hadn't been able to keep their hands off each other. A time when passion had sizzled in the air and hunger was never sated. But the past was as ephemeral as the trade winds, blowing through her heart and mind and passing all too quickly.

"What exactly is it that you want from me, Rico?"

"I want *you,*" he said flatly.

The ice inside her melted in a flash, dwarfed by a rush of heat that boiled her blood and fried her bones. "You what?"

"I want you here," he said, leaning casually against the railing. Feet crossed at the ankles, arms folded across his chest, he added plainly, "In my bed."

"You do?" Had she read him completely wrong? Had he really kept their marriage alive because he still felt something for her? Was this his way of telling her that he wanted them to be together again?

"For one month," he qualified, splintering whatever

rainbow-and-unicorn thoughts that were still revolving through her mind.

"What?"

"You heard me," he said. "And you're lucky I'm not demanding the *five years* that you were gone."

She blinked.

"You will stay here for one month. You will share my bed like a good wife."

"You are *not* going to blackmail me into sex."

"Of course not. But we will sleep in the same bed. And when we *do* have sex again, Teresa, it will be your idea," he said, giving her a knowing smile. "You remember how good it was between us…"

Oh, she really did.

"So blackmail won't be necessary."

He was probably right, God help her.

"As I was saying," Rico continued, "at the end of that month, your brother returns my property and I let you go—with a *real* divorce this time. More," he added when she opened her mouth to speak, "I'll give you the evidence I hold against the Coretti family. You can destroy it yourself."

Wow. Her brain had a lot to sift through: everything he'd said, the cold way he'd said it and the right way to react. Her thoughts tumbled over each other in a crash of confusion until she was finally able to concentrate on the single word that stood out from the rest.

"Destroy?" she asked. "You'd turn it all over to me?"

"I will," he assured her, then lifted one shoulder in a casual shrug. "And I don't lie."

She frowned at the little slap, but instead of arguing the point, she turned her mind to what he'd promised. If she could destroy any evidence on her family, the Corettis would be safe again. But as her father had said, no one before Rico had ever managed to catch them in the act. How could she be sure that Rico had what he said he did?

"How do I know you have anything for us to worry about?"

"As you told your father not long ago, I don't bluff." He pushed away from the railing. "I have enough on them to make any law enforcement agency do a dance of joy as they close a cell door on your father and brothers."

A knot tightened in the pit of her stomach. Rico was a man who said what he meant and always meant what he said. If he promised retribution, then it would be delivered with a vengeance. If he said he could lock her family away, the cell door was as good as shut.

Her heart felt as if it were being squeezed by a cold fist. Looking into his eyes only made the chill she felt go deeper. Though he stood no more than three feet from her, the distance separating them could just as easily have been measured in light-years. "This is about revenge, then?"

"Absolutely." He smiled, but it was an empty echo of the smile she remembered. The smile that still haunted her dreams. "Did you expect me to declare my love? To have spent the last five years pining away for the woman who stole from me and vanished?"

"Pining away?" she repeated with a short laugh. "Please. I've seen the pictures of you in the magazines. Actresses. Models. Socialites. You didn't look like you were crying on their shoulders, either."

One corner of his mouth quirked. "Jealous?"

Desperately. "Hardly."

His gaze narrowed on her. "A thief from a family of thieves. Why should I believe you?"

"I didn't steal from you," she argued, beginning to feel a flutter of outrage building inside.

"Your family did, which makes you as guilty as they."

Okay, she had to give him that. She was a Coretti, after all, despite the fact that she'd never taken part in one of their jobs. "So it's revenge on my entire family that you're after?"

"No, Teresa," he said, moving closer, lifting one hand to cup her cheek. The tender touch was muted by the hard glint in his eyes. "From your family, I want only my property. From you…I want only the pleasure we'll find together during the next month."

Everything inside her rippled and pulsed. Just those few words were enough to build a fire in her blood. How was it fair that he had been with countless women over the last five years while she had lived like a nun? How was it fair that he could whisper the word *pleasure* and have her ready to fall into bed with him?

"And if I'm not interested in sex with you?" she asked, with a mental *hah!* "Would you force me?"

His blue eyes flashed a warning. "You think I would— *could* do that?"

"No," she murmured, shaking her head for emphasis. "I don't."

He nodded. "Good."

"But," she said quickly, "apparently you're not above blackmailing me into your bed."

"You're my *wife*. You belong in bed with me. And as I've told you, I don't have to blackmail you into sex. Soon, you'll be *begging* me to take you," Rico told her with a smile. "And I will be happy to acquiesce. Think of it. You spend the month with me and I don't see your family locked away."

"I don't remember you being so hard…" Her words trailed off as she shook her head sadly.

"A lot has changed in the last five years," he told her.

Her eyes were golden-brown and dreamy, just as he remembered them. Her scent was the same, too, faintly floral with a hint of summer nights. His hands itched to hold her and he told himself he was just eager to get started on the revenge for which he'd waited so long.

But it was more than that and he knew it.

The memory of this one woman had tormented him enough that no other woman had ever come close to erasing Teresa from his mind. It was time now to exorcise that memory so he could move the hell on.

"Do you agree to my terms?" He asked the question because he wanted to hear her say yes. He wasn't the kind of man to take a woman against her will—and it pissed him off that she could even suggest it to him. But he wasn't above making sure the woman he desired didn't have much choice, either. At least in Teresa's case.

She was the only woman who had stayed with him, thoughts of her eating away at him day and night. And it wasn't just her betrayal that made her so unforgettable. No, it was more than that, though the fact that she'd lied to him and used him gnawed at Rico constantly.

She was the woman who had made him *feel* more than he ever had. Hell, he'd *married* her when he had been sure that he'd never want to be with one woman for the rest of his life. With Teresa, though, he hadn't second-guessed anything. He'd listened to his heart and thought her a gift. He'd married her because he hadn't been able to imagine his life without her. He'd let down his guard around her and had ended up paying for that.

After she had vanished, he'd figured out that she hadn't been a gift, but a curse. Now he was going to get past the old anger and sense of betrayal. He was going to use her to pave his way to the future.

A future *without* Teresa Coretti.

"So?" he asked, a casualness he didn't feel coloring his tone. "What is it going to be, Teresa? Do you stay with me for a month or do you wave goodbye to your family as the jail doors slam shut?"

She lifted her chin, fixed her gaze on his and whispered, "I'll stay."

Teresa was surprised Rico had let her out of his sight.

Although, she told herself an hour later, maybe she shouldn't have been. He knew all too well that she wouldn't do anything to endanger her family. So of course she would agree to his terms. And of course she wouldn't make a break for freedom. And of course she would end up having sex with him. How could she not? Teresa had been dreaming about Rico for five years. Sleeping beside him wouldn't be enough and she knew it as well as he did.

She walked along the dock, headed for the boat launch where her father and brother waited. Rico had made arrangements for her family to be taken from the island to St. Thomas. From there, they could take a plane back to Italy and hopefully retrieve Rico's dagger from Gianni's collection. Thankfully, her brother hadn't sold the dagger, as he did most things the Coretti family liberated from their owners. Gianni had a small, priceless collection of his own and she knew that dagger was a part of it.

In one month, her family would be back to return the antiquity and free Teresa.

A soft breeze caressed her and tossed a long lock of her hair across her eyes. She plucked it free, plastered a fake smile on her face and studied her family as she approached them.

Her father was cool and calm—nothing shattered the reserve Dominick wore as elegantly as the three-piece suits he preferred. But Paulo looked agitated. He paced back and forth in front of their father, gesticulating wildly and arguing. Though his words were caught by the wind and carried away from her, Teresa had no problem guessing what he was saying. He was furious and she knew that her brother in a temper was someone to avoid. Though there was no chance of that now. She had to face them both, give them Rico's ultimatum and then watch them go.

"Cara," her father murmured as she came closer. "You're leaving with us after all?"

"No, Papa," she said and withstood the urge to throw herself into her father's arms for a hug she badly needed. "I'm staying here."

"For how long?" Paulo demanded.

"A month."

"Hell with that!"

She looked up at her older brother and winced when she saw just how angry he was. He was tall and dark and right now his brown eyes were flashing with fury. "Paulo, you being mad isn't helping me."

"I'm supposed to just accept this?" he asked. "Just leave you here with that man for a month?"

"Yeah. We all have to accept it." Reaching out, she gave Paulo a brief hug and felt better when he squeezed her back. Paulo and Gianni had always looked out for her. Since she was the baby of the family *and* a girl, it was to be expected, she supposed. So naturally Paulo would have a hard time seeing her caught in a web he couldn't get her out of.

"Like it or not," she said, looking from her brother to her father, "Rico is still my husband."

"Yeah, and I want to know how *that* happened," Paulo muttered.

"Me, as well," her father said.

"I'll tell you everything when I leave here, okay?" Teresa took a deep breath and blew it out in a rush. "Look, the important thing to remember is that Rico won't hurt me."

"No, just trap you."

"Paulo…"

"Color this any way you choose, Teresa," her brother said, "but the hard truth is, he's using *us* to get you back into his bed."

She winced and tried not to look at her father. Maybe Paulo was right—but what her brother didn't know was that Teresa was torn about her own reaction to the situation. Yes, Rico wanted his dagger back, but was it also possible that he wanted *her,* too, even if he couldn't admit it to himself?

"Surely not," Dominick muttered.

"Why else would he keep her here for a month?" Paulo threw his hands high in disgust. "He knows we could get hold of Gianni and have that damned dagger back here by tomorrow. He's doing this deliberately. To keep Teresa where he wants her."

"This is not acceptable," her father said shortly.

"Papa, we're *married.*"

"This does not give him the right to—"

Thankfully, he didn't finish the sentence. There was

only so much more Teresa could take today. Besides, she knew Rico well enough to know that nothing would change his mind. Firing a glare at her big brother, she said, "One month. Then you can return the dagger Gianni stole and Rico will let me leave. *With* the evidence he's gathered about us."

Paulo pushed one hand through his hair. "I still don't like it."

"I don't either," she admitted, "but we don't have a choice."

"I won't leave you here with him," her father said softly. "I won't use my child to bargain for my own safety."

"What Papa said," Paulo muttered. "If your ex wants to throw us in jail, let him."

She loved them both for wanting to make the sacrifice, but she couldn't allow it. "You'd all go to prison for years."

"But you didn't do anything wrong," Paulo argued. "Not right that you should be the one to pay this price."

Teresa fought down a tide of guilt that seemed to swell up from the bottom of her heart. If that were true, she thought, she wouldn't be in this mess in the first place. She had been wrong. She'd lied to Rico from the beginning and then she'd run away rather than tell him the truth.

"Gianni stole the dagger, that's true," she said, with a glance over her shoulder at the Tesoro Castle up on the hill behind her. "But I'm not entirely innocent in this either."

"This doesn't feel right, Teresa," Paulo told her, "leaving you here. With *him*."

Shaking her head, she looked back at her brother. "He's still my husband, remember?"

Her father gave her a long look. "Not for much longer."

"One month, Papa. I'll tell you everything at the end of the month."

One of the island's launch boats fired up its engine, shattering the quiet and bringing home the fact that soon Teresa would be alone with a man who'd waited five years for revenge. Sadly, she was both concerned about that…and aroused.

Talking to her family again, she said, "Don't worry. I'm not in any danger. Rico's angry, but he would never hurt me."

"He's keeping you here against your will," her father reminded her.

"I'm staying because I choose to stay, Papa," she said.

He frowned, glanced at the launch boat that would take them to St. Thomas, then turned back to her. "We've already tried to call Gianni. He's not answering his phone. We'll find him, though, and get the dagger your *husband* requires."

Briefly, she wondered where her oldest brother had vanished to this time. Gianni hadn't been around much in the last couple of years and when he did spend time with the family, he was even more secretive than usual.

"Wait a month before returning, Papa. Rico means what he says."

"I will wait," Nick answered with a hard look at Paulo, who was grumbling under his breath. "If you're sure you want to do this."

Want was a strong word, she thought. Oh, she *wanted* Rico, there was no denying that. But if she had any real choice, would she choose to stay with a man who could barely stand to look at her? Probably not. But the truth was, they were all out of options.

"I'm sure," she said and hoped her voice sounded stronger than she felt at the moment.

"I still don't like it," Paulo muttered.

"Neither do I," their father agreed, then stepped close enough to draw his daughter into the circle of his arms. He held her tightly for a long moment and Teresa snuggled in, taking the comfort he offered before he leaned back to look at her. "You are the one who decided to not be a part of the family business, Teresa. It is not right that you are the one to pay for your legacy."

She forced a smile she didn't feel. "It's only a month, Papa. Then I'll really be free. And so will my family. That's all that matters."

He huffed out an exasperated breath then snapped, "Take the bags to the boat."

With a last look at his sister, Paulo scooped up their luggage and headed down the dock.

"You're certain you'll be safe here?"

"I will," she lied. Of course, she wasn't worried about Rico actually *hurting* her. Not physically, anyway. But every time he looked at her through eyes that spat fury, a new emotional wound opened up inside her.

Nodding, Nick looked up to the white hotel on the crest of the hill behind them, as if he could see straight into Rico's eyes. When he turned back to his daughter, he sighed. "I should have listened to you, *cara,* about staying away from this man. I swear to you now, when this month is over, Rico King will be nothing but a bad memory. For all of us."

He had never been a *bad* memory to Teresa, though. And she knew that after another month with him, most likely spent in his bed, she would never again be able to pry him out of her mind. But her father didn't need to know that her heart was still uncertain when it came to the man who was now pulling their strings like a master puppeteer.

"It'll be fine, Papa."

Still frowning, he nodded. Then he kissed her forehead and stepped back. "One month, Teresa. We will come back for you in one month."

She nodded too, though her heart was breaking. Her family was leaving and any minute now she would be alone with the one man who could shatter her heart and soul. "I'll see you then."

She watched them board the small craft and stood on the dock, gaze locked on the boat until it was no more than a smudge on the horizon. Then she turned and stared up at Rico's castle—wondering what kind of dungeon he had in store for her.

Four

A half hour later, her family had left the island and Teresa was exactly where Rico wanted her. In the bedroom of the home he'd had built for himself on the island. Just beyond the hotel, there was a rise of land that overlooked the ocean on one side and the forest on another. Rico had known the moment he'd seen it that this was where he would build his house.

And though he had furnished it and staffed it and lived in it for almost a year now—it had felt empty to him until today. Now *she* was here and the palatial home felt…crowded.

He watched her walk around the room, stepping tentatively, as if she expected land mines to be lying beneath the gleaming bamboo floor. White linen curtains rippled and danced in the island breeze that wafted through the open windows. Birds in the trees beyond sang in harmonies that lent a peaceful air to this confrontation that was *anything* but peaceful.

In her red silk shirt and dark blue slacks, she looked like a jewel dropped from the sky against the background of his room's white walls and furnishings. He waited for her to speak. To say *something* about what had happened five years before. Hell, to beg him to release her. But she gave him nothing, and a part of him wasn't surprised.

Narrowing his gaze on her, he blurted out, "Was it all a lie? Right from the beginning?"

She turned so quickly her dark hair swung out around her in a curtain of silky movement. "What do you want me to say?"

Tricky question.

"I want the truth, but somehow I doubt I'll get it," Rico said, never taking his gaze off the woman across the room from him.

"Then why should I say anything?" she countered. "You wouldn't believe whatever I told you."

How the hell could he? He kept his distance purposely. He didn't quite trust himself when he was too close to her. The need in him roared for satisfaction and the anger was just as raw.

Oh, he'd never hurt her. He didn't hurt women. But damn it, he didn't want to blackmail her into staying with him, either. Damn her for bringing him to this. And damn her for putting him here, in this position. Soon enough, though, he would have her panting to have him making love to her once again. Then he would remind her just what she'd given up by disappearing so long ago.

No other person in the world had managed to twist Rico up like she had. She'd dug so deeply inside him, there was no room for anyone else. He had his family, of course. The Kings were loyal down to the bone.

But there hadn't been another woman in his life since Teresa and his body was clamoring for what he'd denied it for too damn long.

Sure, he'd gone out with women. Had even brought a few of them back to his rooms at the hotel. But he'd never brought one to his home before. Never taken one into his bed. Not since Teresa.

He knew what it looked like to the world at large, but the world saw what it wanted to see. A billionaire playboy. The man with a succession of gorgeous women on his arm. But those women never touched him. Never shared his bed. And none of them would admit to it, because none of them could stand letting the public know that *they* hadn't been able to coax a King into their beds.

So as Teresa had lied to him, Rico had lived a lie for five long years and now that the end was in sight, he wanted her so badly he was hard as stone. So yeah, better he keep his distance.

"Try me. Tell me why. Why any of it?"

"Telling you why won't change anything, Rico. Why go there?"

"We never *left* there."

She shrugged and walked to the French doors opposite his bed that led to the terrace. She stared out and he knew the view she was looking at. The white sand beach. The aquamarine ocean beyond. The banyan trees and the double-wide hammock strung between them. There was a stone patio out there, surrounded by so many different varieties of flowers it took the breath away even as it urged you to breathe deeply, to savor the scents and tastes on the wind. There was a boat at his private dock, a yacht that Rico took out when he needed complete privacy and time to think. And when it was still and quiet enough, you could hear the waterfall in the nearby forest that splashed over rocks worn smooth by time and the relentless rush of the river.

He'd built his treasure, his paradise on Tesoro. And now that she was here—it felt complete.

"There's nothing I can say to you, Rico."

"There's plenty you could have said five years ago," he countered.

She blew out a breath and shook her head. "If I give you a reason, will it make this better for you?"

Nothing would. Nothing could. "Give it a shot."

"Fine," she said, crossing her arms over her chest in a classic self-defensive posture. "I slept with you because you were gorgeous. Famous. Rich. What girl wouldn't go to bed with you?"

A fresh spurt of anger shot through him even as he identified the lie in her words. She was too dismissive. Too careless to be telling him any kind of truth. But this lie would serve him as no truth could.

"Good. Then the next month will be easy for you," he said, at last crossing the room in long, slow strides that had her automatically backing away. "I'm still famous. Still rich. So being with me again won't be a hardship for you."

He saw her pale slightly. Then she stiffened her spine and squared her shoulders.

"I'm ready to pay my debt." She glanced at the bed, then to him. "Now?"

God, yes.

"No." He enjoyed the flicker of surprise he caught in her eyes. "I've already told you, I don't bargain for sex,

Teresa. When we come together again, it will be because you *need* me. Not because you are paying a bill owed by your family." She flushed and the color was lovely on her skin.

By the time he was finished with her, she'd be pleading with him to take her. "Your things have been brought here from your suite at the hotel."

"Here? To your house?"

"Here. To my *room*," he corrected. "Our room—for the next month, anyway."

She stiffened her spine but flattened her lips together to keep from saying whatever was stuck in her throat. Didn't matter, he told himself. Nothing mattered now. Nothing but finally getting the revenge he'd promised himself so long ago. And still, he had to ask. "One more question."

"Only one?"

"Were you planning your family's theft from the beginning?"

"Would it matter if I said no?"

He thought about that for a second or two. "No, because how could I believe a thief?"

She winced and he almost felt guilty—almost.

"Get dressed. We're going to dinner."

She frowned and couldn't stop herself from asking, "Dinner?"

Her surprise told him he had caught her off guard. Good. Now all he had to do was keep her there. "Be ready in an hour."

After he left Teresa in his room, Rico stalked down the long hallway leading to the front of the house. He didn't notice the throw rugs in bright tropical colors or the sunlight glancing in through the front windows to lie on the gleaming tile floor. His mind was too busy, his emotions choking him too completely to be interested in the mundane. Right now all he could think about was the fact that Teresa was back with him. And what that was going to mean.

In long strides, he marched down the long, elegant hallway directly to the library. Once there, he sealed himself inside, walked to his desk and sat down behind it. Snatching up the phone, he hit the speed dial and waited for the connection to be made.

"Hello?"

His cousin Sean's voice sounded clipped and a little harassed. Rico smiled. "Catch you at a bad time, Sean?"

A huff of resignation came before Sean King said, "No. Just recovering from my latest heart attack. Mel had another false alarm."

In spite of everything going on, Rico had to grin. Sean King had, since marrying Melinda Stanford, become a changed man. Wasn't so long ago that Sean himself would have laughed at the image of himself as devoted husband and father-to-be. Now, though, he was the prototypical family man. And since Melinda's due date was only a week or two away, he never let his wife out of his sight. Every sigh she made sent Sean into a tailspin, and watching his anxiety escalate over the last several months had been *very* entertaining. While Melinda was sailing through her pregnancy, it was about to kill Sean.

"I swear," Sean said under his breath, "sometimes I think Mel's doing it on purpose. I'm sitting here watching the game and she lets out this little whimper-slash-groan. I jumped up so fast I knocked my beer over and dumped a whole bowl of popcorn on the floor. The dog loves me."

Rico laughed. "If it's this bad before she goes into labor, how will you survive the real thing?"

"Once it actually *happens* I'll be fine," Sean argued. "It's this waiting and waiting that's making me nuts. And between you and me, I think Mel's doing this stuff just to watch me jump."

She probably was. Melinda was great, but she did love keeping her husband on his toes. "I'm sure she's as nervous as you are."

"Who's nervous?" Sean replied. "I'm not nervous. I'm just hyperprepared." He grumbled something under his breath then added, "Right now, she's eating ice cream and laughing at me."

In the background, Rico could hear Melinda's laughter and the excited barking of their dog, Herman. Soon they would have their child and be even happier than they were already. Hard not to be jealous of that.

"You're a lucky man," Rico told him.

"Yeah, and she never lets me forget it," Sean said, laughing. "So what's going on?"

Secrets were impossible to keep inside the King family. So naturally Rico's brothers and cousins all knew about his marriage to Teresa—and the fact that the divorce had never gone through. Hell, with a lot of the Kings now living across Europe, Rico had had unpaid "detectives" keeping their eyes open looking for Teresa so that Rico could finally end what was still lying between them.

The King family was tight. And since Sean had led the King Construction project to build this hotel and Rico's home—then stayed on Tesoro when he married Melinda—the two cousins had grown even closer. They'd spent many nights having a drink together, talking about work and family and what Rico would do if he ever caught up to Teresa Coretti King.

Now that he finally had, Rico had to talk to his cousin about this. He took a breath and said simply, "She's back."

"She?"

"Teresa."

There was a long pause and Rico knew his cousin was as dumbstruck as he'd been just a couple of hours ago. Idly, he picked up a pen off the desktop and flipped it between his fingers.

"Are you kidding me?" Sean's voice ratcheted up a notch or two before he stopped and talked to Melinda. "Rico's wife showed up. Yeah, I'm finding out." When he came back, he asked, "She just showed up at the hotel?"

"Not alone. She was with her father and brother—who were doing what they do best."

"Oh, crap. They were pulling jobs on your guests?"

"Yeah. Serenity James lost a necklace and there were a few others hit, as well." Just thinking about it infuriated Rico all over again. Of course he'd made sure the Corettis turned over the stolen property before they left the island, but the fact that thefts had occurred at all seriously pissed him off. "They returned the jewels before they left."

"Before you tossed 'em off the island, you mean."

"That's about it."

"And you didn't alert the police because…"

"Because I made a deal with Teresa."

"Oh, man, do I want to know what it is?"

Rico tossed the pen to the desktop and watched it roll off the far edge. Leaning back in his chair, he outlined his plan for revenge and waited for Sean's reaction. It didn't take long.

"So basically you took her prisoner?" A yelp from Melinda in the background caused Sean to say, "I know, Mel. I'm finding out." Then he asked, "Okay, so where's Teresa now?"

"In my bedroom."

"Oh, for God's sake, Rico—"

"She's still my wife, Sean." He prepared for a battle. He'd talked to his cousin many times about the frustration he'd felt over the years. Now that his revenge was at hand, though, Rico almost felt…guilty about wielding it. So he'd called his cousin for some backup. Which, it appeared, he wasn't going to get.

"She's your wife but you haven't seen her in five years."

"You don't have to remind me," Rico said, flipping the pen between his fingers.

"So what're you planning to do? Lock her up?" Sean asked. "Chain her to the bed?"

"I hadn't considered it, but…" Now that erotic image seared itself on his brain as he considered it.

Fine. He was kidding. Probably. Although the thought of Teresa chained to his bed awakened a mental image that suddenly made him completely uncomfortable. Pushing out of his chair, Rico paced the perimeter of the room. Even the air of home seemed different now, with Teresa here. She was just up the stairs and it was taking everything he had to keep from storming up there. He knew she would see his hunger for her, but it would only mirror what she was feeling and push her closer to coming to him.

Sean sighed. "What's the plan?"

"Just what I said." Rico stopped at the wide front window overlooking the meticulously landscaped front yard.

"She stays with me for one month. Then her family returns the dagger and I divorce her."

"Uh-huh." Sean blew out a breath. "Until that happens, what're you gonna do with her?"

He knew what he *wanted* to do with her. His body was rock hard and just knowing Teresa was upstairs, in a room with a wide, comfortable bed, made even breathing difficult. But he had time. His wife would be here, with him, for a solid month and in that time he would find a way to finally and completely get Teresa out of his mind for good.

But for now, "We're going to dinner at the hotel."

Sean snorted. "Sure. When your missing wife reappears after five years of running from you, you want to put off revenge long enough to have a dinner date."

"It's not a date." Even the word had Rico scowling.

"Then what is it?"

"It's dinner." Rico slapped one hand to the wall beside the window and glared out at his yard. "I'm not romancing her. I'm not courting her. We both have to eat and I don't want her out of my sight. Don't make more of this than there is, Sean."

"Sure, sure. Not a date. Just revenge foreplay. Got it all planned out, huh?" There was a distinctive smile in Sean's voice that irritated Rico beyond measure.

"Is there something wrong with a plan?"

"Nope," Sean said. "Just be prepared, cousin."

"For what?"

"For when your plan blows up in your face."

Teresa's stomach was in knots. Just being with Rico was tearing her up. And waiting for whatever was going to happen next was making her a little crazy. Who knew what he would do? She never would have expected to be held hostage and since he'd surprised her once, she had to wonder what else was ticking through his mind.

Oh, she had known the minute she slipped from their suite at the Castello de King five years ago that she had made him her enemy. It had broken her heart at the time, but over the last five years, she had tried to heal. Tried to forget the fact that she had run away from a man who had loved her. And though her inner wounds had healed over, the scar tissue was still tender. Being here with him now, Teresa knew that even more pain was headed her way. There was no chance to avoid it. When this month with him was over, that was it. All dreams would be dead. All hope gone.

So should she treat this month as the punishment Rico considered it—or should she embrace it and pack in as many memories as she could? Enough to last her a lifetime?

"If I turn this around," she whispered into the quiet room, "and look at this month as a gift from the fates…" What? She wouldn't be in pain later? She'd get the happy ending to her fairy tale?

"No," she told herself, refusing to even begin to blow a bubble of hope that was doomed to burst. "But at least this time with him will be easier. For both of us."

She almost laughed. Nothing about this was going to be easy, no matter how she colored it. The man she had loved so desperately wanted her—but only for the revenge she could provide. There was no happily ever after in her future. But she still had the choice to either accept this coming month as he'd described it—a punishment—or to look at it as one last thing she could share with Rico.

The door to the bedroom opened on a hush of sound

and she turned to look at the man standing in the doorway. He took her breath away. In this palace of tropical pastel colors and varying shades of white, he stood apart. Dressed entirely in black—slacks, long-sleeved shirt, shoes—he looked…dangerous. And she knew he was. At least, to her own sensibility. His black hair was too long, curling around the collar of his shirt. His blue eyes shone against his tan. His mouth was a grim slash. He tucked his hands into the pockets of his slacks, leaned one shoulder against the doorjamb and fixed his gaze on her.

She felt that look as surely as she would have a touch. Heat washed through her and her breath came in short, sharp gasps. Oh, she was in very deep trouble here. And she couldn't even really regret that he had ensured she stay with him. How could she? She'd missed him for five years. Now that she was with him again, how could she *not* enjoy it?

"You're ready. Good. We're leaving." He straightened up, turned and walked out of the room, clearly expecting her to follow.

She glanced into the mirror and gave herself a quick look. She was wearing a lemon-yellow dress, with narrow straps over her shoulders, a deeply cut back and a full skirt that ended just above her knees. Her long black hair was drawn back into a tumble of curls that fell down between her shoulder blades and the gold hoops at her ears winked in the light. She looked good and she knew it.

Yet Rico had almost looked *through* her. As if he hadn't seen her at all. As if she was no more important to him than any of the other furnishings in his lovely home.

She was nothing to him now.

And so the pain began.

* * *

Once they were at his hotel, Rico stalked across the main dining room. He kept one hand at Teresa's back as if to assure himself she wouldn't bolt. But the feel of her bare skin beneath his palm was a fire that wouldn't be denied. Heat spilled up his arm and through his chest to spread lower until simply walking was an agony. The low back of her dress showcased the pale honey tone of her smooth skin and made a man's gaze dip lower, to the curve of her behind. Then Rico's mind took over, just to drive him completely around the bend.

Nice job, he told himself silently. *You're supposed to be punishing her and instead, you're torturing yourself.* Yeah. This month was going to be a piece of cake.

While the maître d' hustled to escort them to his private table, Rico's gaze slipped around the room. Black tablecloths, candles on every table, the flames flickering in the soft wind drifting in through the opened windows that allowed the scent of flowers to wash over the room. Muted conversations, the clink of crystal and classical music being pumped through the stereo system all came together to make King's Castle on Tesoro's dining room the elegant sanctuary it was. Waiters moved swiftly, silently through the maze of tables. Champagne corks popped, wine was poured and the finest food in the world was served. He had built this, following the vision he'd had to create a lush, sensual retreat. A place where reality took a backseat and dreams came to life. Where sensual pleasures were enhanced and fantasies sprang to life.

Now he himself was caught up in one of those fantasies.

He noticed the furtive glances of other men as they

passed and he knew they were admiring Teresa. Well, hell, who could blame them? She was beautiful, but more, there was an inherent pride in the way she held herself. The tilt of her chin, the flash in her eyes. He knew they saw all of that, because he had seen the same the first time he met her—when he had known he had to have her.

That need was as fresh tonight as it had been so long ago.

The booth at the back of the restaurant had a view of the entire room, yet remained set apart. Private. *His*. He felt her shiver as they stepped into the shadows and he hid a smile. He liked knowing that she was off balance. Rico had the power here and he wasn't going to give it up. Sensing Teresa's nerves smoothed the jagged surfaces of the simmering anger and raw need clawing at Rico's insides.

She gave the maître d' a smile and then slid across the burgundy leather seat. Rico's heartbeat skittered wildly, but he buried the reaction to her smile and told the tuxedoed man beside him, "Champagne."

"Right away." He scurried off and Rico slid into the booth beside Teresa.

"Champagne?" she asked.

"We're celebrating, aren't we?" He leaned back and laid one arm across the back of the bench seat. "After all, it's been five years. A reunion deserves champagne, don't you think?"

"Reunion." She laughed a little under her breath, but the sound didn't mask her anxiety. "Is that what this is?"

"You have been in the wind for five years, Teresa," he said, his voice low enough that only she could possibly hear him. "I think we both deserve to mark this… *occasion*."

In seconds, a waiter appeared tableside and uncorked the champagne. After pouring some for Rico and getting a nod of approval, he poured two glasses and then disappeared, leaving them alone again.

Teresa took a long sip, then sat back, closed her eyes and sighed.

That soft, breathy sound shot through Rico like a bullet. His body was hard as stone and his mind was struggling to keep the memory of her betrayal sharp and clear so that his body and heart couldn't surrender again. He'd already lived through that once. He wouldn't do it again.

"I'm surprised your father agreed to the deal I offered him."

Her eyes opened and brown eyes met blue. "Did you think he wouldn't?"

He shrugged. "I have no idea how a thief thinks."

She sucked in a breath. "Are you going to be throwing that word around for the whole month?"

"It's appropriate, don't you think?" He paused for a sip of his champagne and let the bubbles slide down his throat. In the flickering candlelight, her golden-brown eyes glittered. "If not for your family's occupation, we wouldn't be here."

Her eyes never left his face. "And you'll never let me forget it."

"Why would I?" He set the crystal flute down and stared at her, meeting her accusing glare with one of his own. He was the one who had been cheated, lied to, stolen from. How she had the nerve to act like the injured party was beyond him. But he wasn't going to let her get away with it. "You don't like the word *thief*? Which would you prefer? Criminal? Burglar? Or perhaps *cat burglar* would be more specific."

Her fingers swept up and down the slender stem of her champagne flute. His gaze caught the motion and fixated on it. He imagined that small, dainty hand sliding across his body and it took everything he had not to reach out and grab her. Drag her to him across the bench seat and haul her across his lap where she could *feel* what she was doing to his body. He wanted his hands on her again. He needed to feel the flash and heat of her body against his.

This month was either going to satisfy his need for payback—or kill him.

"The Coretti family has been doing what they do for generations."

Just like that, it was as if ice water had been poured in his lap.

"And that makes it all right?"

"I didn't say that."

"You used me for your family's sake and then left when the job was finished."

Her eyes went soft and then hard again in a blink. As if she'd deliberately shut out whatever it was that had caused that momentary weakness. "I've told you. I didn't know they were going to take the dagger until the job was done."

"Very convenient."

"Nothing convenient about it," she muttered, then lifted her chin and met his gaze squarely. "If you think it was easy for me to leave you, you're crazy."

"Easy or not, you did it," he said and as memory and anger roared into life inside him, his accent became more pronounced. He heard it in his whispered words, but couldn't seem to tame it. "I have never been used before or since. That makes you *special,* Teresa. And I won't rest until you've returned my property and paid for what you did."

"I have paid," she told him and her voice sounded unbelievably weary. "For five years, I've paid for what I did, Rico. But it doesn't matter what I say, does it? You won't believe me."

"No," he agreed. "I won't. That's the downside of being a liar. Even when you claim to be telling the truth, no one will listen."

How the hell could he? She'd ripped him in two when she disappeared. Never before or since had he allowed a woman to slip into his life as Teresa Coretti had. She'd crept past his defensive shields and burrowed her way into his heart. His soul. In the short time they were together, she'd given him more than he had ever hoped to find.

Then she'd been gone.

And the cold that had filled him once he'd learned that she and her family had used him had never really ebbed. Being beside her now, he felt sexual heat, but even that wasn't enough to burn off the stinging chill of the memory of her betrayal.

All around them, couples leaned across tables, laughing and talking in soft murmurs that added to the romance of the room. But here at his table, there was a distance between him and Teresa that might as well have been a brick wall.

"Then why are we here?" she asked after several long moments of silence. "If you don't want to talk to me or hear my side of things, why didn't you just lock me in your bedroom?"

Good question. But the answer wasn't one he was ready to give her. How could he admit to her that having her standing there in his room had pushed every one of his buttons? She'd been too close, the situation too intimate. He'd needed time. Time to think about exactly how he wanted this to go. Time to get his own raging need under control. Because he wouldn't be led around by his sexual desire. This time, where Teresa was concerned, he wouldn't allow his brain to be clouded by desire.

"Have to eat." His tone was dismissive and the sentence short and sharp. He wanted her to know that it didn't matter to him that she was sitting beside him smelling like hot summer nights.

"Fine. We'll eat." She took another long drink of her champagne, then sighed heavily. "Then maybe you can tell me exactly what you expect of me for the next month."

His body stirred. Oh, he expected plenty. "I think you already know."

She closed her eyes briefly. "I suppose I do. Not getting enough action from the models and actresses you squire around?"

One eyebrow arched. "Been keeping track of me? Flattering."

"Not really," she said with a sniff. "It's hard not to know what you're up to when you're splashed across magazines and newspapers—complete with pictures of you and the bimbo of the week."

"My life is none of your business." He scowled at her and left it at that. He didn't care for the disapproval in her voice. She was the one who had walked out. Who was she to pass judgment on anything he did? Let her think what she would. Her opinion of him meant less than nothing, didn't it?

"You're right. It's not my business. But answer one question for me. Why didn't you just let me go five years ago? Why stop the divorce and go to the trouble of sending me a forged decree?"

His fingers clenched around the delicate crystal stem and Rico had to force his grip to relax before the glass simply shattered in his hand. When he finally spoke, his voice was low and even, despite the anger churning within.

"You ran. From *me*." His gaze caught hers and he noticed the flicker of...was it shame shining in her light brown eyes? If so, he was glad to see it. "I'm a King, Teresa. We don't lose. Ever."

She pulled in a long, shuddering breath. "So this is a game? A competition? I can leave but only when *you* say so?"

"If this is a game, it is one you devised," he reminded her. "But it is one I will win."

"You're wrong," Teresa said softly, with a slow shake of her head. "No one's going to win."

His heart fisted in his chest and that tight knot of pain told him she was probably right. By the time they were through, there would be no winners.

Only survivors.

"Are we interrupting?"

He knew that voice. Scowling, Rico turned to the man standing beside his table. He slanted a hard look at his cousin Sean, then smiled at the lovely, *very* pregnant woman by his side.

"Would it matter if I said yes?" Rico asked his cousin.

"No," Sean said.

"Yes." Melinda spoke up at the same time. She gave her husband's arm a light swat, then shrugged and looked at Teresa. "We are interrupting, but honestly, I just had to get out of the house."

Sean wore slacks and a long-sleeved white shirt. Melinda's long black hair was pulled back into a ponytail gathered at the base of her neck. Her blue eyes looked tired and she was dressed in a long skirt and a clingy top that emphasized her pregnancy.

"You mentioned you were going to dinner," Sean put in, already helping Melinda slide across the leather seat. "And we thought that sounded like a great idea."

He settled at the end of the booth, directly opposite Rico, and gave him a grin. Rico blew out a sigh, but short of tossing his cousin out, there was no way to get rid of him. Besides, Melinda was much too nice to be treated badly because of her idiot husband.

"Hey, champagne!" Sean spotted the bottle nestled in a silver ice bucket and signaled to a waiter for another glass. Remembering his wife, he also ordered a bottle of sparkling water.

While they waited, Rico looked at Teresa. "This is my cousin Sean King and his beautiful wife, Melinda Stanford King."

"Stanford?" Teresa asked. "Any relation to Walter Stanford? The man who owns this island?"

"He's my grandfather."

Rico watched Teresa curiously as the two women fell into an easy conversation. She had known about Walter Stanford. So she'd done some research on Tesoro before arriving on the island. To help her family? Or to find out more about Rico and where he was living now?

She laughed at something Melinda said and the delicious sound settled over him like a warm blanket. Seeing her now, he wasn't looking at his betrayer, but simply a woman so lovely it took his breath away. And he realized that the tightness in his chest was easing.

Maybe it was a good thing Sean had horned in on dinner. Having the other couple here was definitely easing the tension at the table. Though it would no doubt return when the evening was over and they were back at Rico's house.

"So," Sean asked with a smile as the waiter arrived and poured Melinda a glass of the sparkling water. "What's new?"

Rico glared at him. Sean's sense of humor could be irritating at the best of times. Tonight was not the best of times.

"I should ask that of you," Rico said. "When we spoke earlier, you were watching a game. What made you decide to come here instead?"

"This promised more action than what was happening in that game. Dead boring." He took a sip of champagne, then leaned his head toward his wife. "Besides, Mel's getting a little twitchy. Waiting for the baby to make a move can make you restless. Thought she'd have a good time getting out of the house."

"Please," Melinda said with a laugh. "It wasn't just *me* trying to get out for the evening. You were going stir-crazy."

"Maybe a little," Sean allowed and draped one arm around her shoulders.

Shaking her head at her husband, Melinda turned to Teresa. "Sean tells me you've been living in Europe the last few years. What do you do for a living?"

Rico slanted a look at her and waited for her answer. He, too, was interested in how she'd spent her time the last five years. When he'd known her, she'd been one of the chefs at his Cancún hotel. Had she kept her love for cooking, or had that been part of the ruse she'd used to get close to him? How could she be so familiar to him and yet feel like such a stranger?

Teresa glanced at him briefly, as if she'd guessed what he was thinking. Then she turned her full attention to Melinda. "I'm a chef. I've been working at different restaurants in Europe for the last few years."

Melinda frowned a bit. "No home base?"

"No," Teresa said with another glance at Rico. "I move around a lot."

To avoid being found, no doubt, he thought, even though he wondered why. It wasn't as if she had known he was looking for her. So why hadn't she gone back to her family? The ones who had been important enough to her to betray her husband?

"That sounds great," Melinda said. "I love living on the island. Couldn't imagine being anywhere else." She reached out and caught Sean's hand in hers. "I do love to travel, though, so I envy you that. But I really can't empathize with the chef thing. I'm a terrible cook."

"True," Sean put in. "She made tacos last week and even the dog wouldn't eat them. And he'll eat anything."

"Thank you," Melinda said wryly.

Her husband gave her a hard, fast kiss. "Didn't marry you for your cooking abilities," he said with a grin. "We can hire cooks."

"Thank goodness. Or we'd starve," Melinda put in. "Though right now, I'm looking too well fed to be starving."

"You look gorgeous," Teresa said.

"That's what I've been telling her." Rico smiled gently at his cousin's wife. "A pregnant woman is nothing but beautiful."

"And big," Melinda put in. "Don't forget big."

"When're you due?" Teresa asked.

"Officially? A week." The woman winced and shifted position uncomfortably. "But it feels like any minute to me."

Sean shivered dramatically. "Don't say that. At least wait until we get home again."

Melinda patted his hand. "Sean's practiced making the hospital drive from our house five times."

"Smart," Teresa said.

Rico snorted.

Sean sneered at him.

"The hospital is only ten minutes away," Melinda said with an indulgent smile for her husband.

"There could be traffic," he said, defending himself.

"On Tesoro?" Rico laughed and shook his head at his cousin. "The landmass is so small, if you were on the other side of the island it would still only take you twenty minutes to reach the hospital."

"Fine, fine." Sean poured his wife another glass of sparkling water, then topped off his own champagne. "Just wait until *your* wife is pregnant. Then we'll see how funny you think this is."

Silence dropped over the table with a thud of awkwardness. Teresa winced. Melinda slapped her husband's arm again. Rico frowned and Sean took a deep drink of his champagne. "Going to be a long night."

Five

Going to be a long night.

Sean King's words echoed over and over again in Teresa's mind as she waited in Rico's bedroom hours later. He'd already promised that they would sleep in the same bed. But there was no way she could relax until he was here.

She figured she now knew how a sacrificial virgin must have felt just before being tied to an altar stone. Of course, she was no virgin—that ship had sailed long ago. But the nerves were there. The anxiety about what she should do. He'd said nothing would happen between them unless she initiated it. So. *Should* she?

In spite of the anxiousness holding her in its grip, Teresa was…aroused. And she'd thought that over the years she had managed to bury what she'd felt for Rico. She had never met another man who could stir up her insides with a single look. She had thought that Rico was her one chance at happiness and when she'd left him, she had accepted that she would never have him again.

Now she was here, and Teresa was forced to admit, at least to herself, that the thought of going to bed with Rico again had her body burning in anticipation.

It had been so long since he'd touched her. So long since she'd felt the intimate slide of his body into hers. The mental images crashing through her mind made her legs tremble so badly that she was forced to drop into the closest chair. Teresa took a deep breath and let it out slowly, hoping for calm. Calm, though, was impossible to find.

She looked around his bedroom, noting that the space was done in shades of soothing white, from cream to ivory and every shade in between. There were splashes of color in the paintings on the walls and the jewel-toned pillows stacked on the bed wide enough to qualify as a soccer field. The bamboo floor gleamed like old honey in the soft lighting. The chair she sat in was one of two drawn up before a now cold fireplace of river stone. A table between the chairs held a carafe of lemon water, left there by one of Rico's efficient yet nearly invisible staff.

She poured herself a glass of water and drank half of it down, hoping to ease her dry throat. But there was no help there, either. She wasn't thirsty, she was *needy*.

Oh, she hated to even let that thought race through her mind. Hated knowing that her body and heart were still vulnerable to Rico even after five years.

When she'd first met him, he had been open, warm. He'd drawn her in so easily, sweeping her into an affair and a romance and into marriage before she'd even had time to notice how quickly things were moving between them. Even if she had noticed, she wouldn't have cared. It had all felt so right. As if they'd somehow been fated to find each other. She had *loved* completely, for the first time in her life, and she had hoped it was forever.

Now his warmth was gone, covered by a veneer of ice that put a hard glint in his pale blue eyes, and Teresa knew that she was to blame for the change in him. She set her water glass aside and scrubbed her hands up and down her arms, as if she could chase away the chills dancing along her skin. Despite the sexual heat simmering inside her, the cold sensation of impending disaster just wouldn't dissipate.

"Where is he?" she muttered aloud, more to hear a sound in the stillness than for anything else. "What's he waiting for?"

Why wasn't he storming into the bedroom and finding a way to make her beg for him?

Another rush of heat swamped her and she pushed up from the chair. Her knees were weak, but her will was strong. Whatever game Rico was playing, she wasn't going to cooperate. She refused to sit still and worry herself into what her mother used to call a state. Rico expected her to just sit here in this lush *cell* and await his arrival. No doubt he knew exactly what she was going through and was enjoying it.

"But what choice do you have?" she murmured. "Where could you go, even if you were willing to run away again? You're on an *island,* for heaven's sake."

Even if she could, she wouldn't have run. Not again. Everyone made mistakes, she assured herself, but only really foolish people made the *same* ones over and over again.

Muttering, grumbling and trying to get a grip on her

own skittering hormones, Teresa stepped out of the bedroom onto the flagstone terrace.

Instantly, the flower-scented breeze wrapped itself around her as it rattled the leaves on the surrounding trees, sounding like hushed whispers in the dark. At the edge of Rico's property, the ocean sighed into shore, moonlight shimmering on the surface of the water. It was perfect. Dreamlike. She only wished she wasn't too tense to enjoy it.

"Planning to run again?" Rico asked from behind her.

As she whirled around to face him, he continued, "There's nowhere to go this time, Teresa. You can't get off the island until I *let* you go."

He was backlit by the room behind him and in his black clothes, with his black hair and his face in darkness…he looked like a shadow of doom. He wasn't, though. Because ghosts or shades or whatever you wanted to call them didn't give off heat as Rico did. Even from across the patio, she was dazzled by it.

"I wasn't running," she managed to say. "I was waiting."

"For?" He stepped out of the bedroom and walked across the patio toward her. Moonlight shone in his eyes, but his luscious mouth was a grim line and his body language was anything but relaxed.

"I was waiting for you, Rico, and you know it," she said. "I've been here. Alone. For two hours. Is making me wait part of the thrill for you?"

"Thrill?" He moved in so close, she instinctively took a step back. But the metal railing around the patio stopped her retreat and dug into the small of her back. "You think I'm enjoying this?"

"I think you're loving it," she told him as nerves gave

way to the Italian temper her parents had gifted her with. "You had to wait five years, but you're finally getting back at me."

"Did you expect anything less?"

Had she? On those rare occasions when she'd allowed herself to imagine meeting Rico again, she'd never wondered what he'd say to her. What she could possibly say to him. Her imaginings had been more rich fantasies of desire and the passion that still haunted her. In her dreams, she and Rico hadn't wasted a lot of time *talking*. But she was rapidly discovering that reality was much harder to live with than fantasies.

Teresa stared up into his eyes and knew she was in no position to be angry at him. Though temper still simmered inside her, it was slowly draining away. After all, this was her fault. She was the one who'd lied to him so long ago and those lies had eventually brought them here. To this moment.

"No," she said. "I suppose not."

"Why did you come to Tesoro, Teresa?"

She pushed her hair back from her face with one hand, then let it fall to her side again. "When I realized my father and Paulo had come here, I tried to get them away before you found them. That's all."

"I don't think so." He moved in closer and she leaned back because she couldn't move with the railing pressing against her spine. He slapped both hands down on the iron on either side of her, effectively caging her between his arms, and then bent his head until his eyes were boring into hers. She looked into those so familiar and yet so different eyes and saw nothing soft or tender or loving. All that shone back at her was temper and ice.

"I think you came because you *wanted* me to catch you at last. Because you couldn't stay away."

"You're wrong." She shook her head, determined to deny his words. If he was right, then she was a monumental fool.

"Am I?" His voice dropped to a husky whisper that hinted at intimacy. "You could have phoned your father. Warned your brother to leave. Instead, you came here, to my place."

All right, yes. She could have phoned. Could have tried to talk to her family long-distance from the safety of her apartment in Naples. Oh, she'd told herself that they wouldn't listen to her if she called. That she would have to convince them in person. But what if Rico was right? What if her hunger to be near him again had sent her right into his revenge plan?

Oh, God, she hoped not. Because that would mean her feelings for him were still too rich, too deep for her own good.

"Think about it, Teresa," Rico urged, his mouth just a breath away from hers. "You came to me. And now that I have you…"

Her insides swirled and heat rushed through her in a blink. Her throat went dry and her breath locked in her chest. Funny, but his idea of revenge—keeping her in his bed for a month until she surrendered to the want clamoring inside her—was just what she'd been dreaming about ever since she'd left him. The punishment for her would be when the month was over and he gave her the divorce she had thought she'd gotten years ago.

He brushed his lips across hers. Once. Twice. Just the barest touch of his mouth to hers and fireworks exploded inside her. She shivered and watched as he pulled away, then straightened, taking a step back from her.

"Now that I have you," he repeated, "we do this *my* way."

"What is your way, Rico?"

"That you'll find out soon enough." He turned toward the bedroom. "Come. It's late and I'm tired."

Tired?

She was still struggling for breath as she watched him go. Her knees were rubbery and her head was spinning. Her heart was racing and at the core of her, she felt hot and achy. A barely there kiss had reduced her to this—and hadn't seemed to affect Rico at all.

She was tangled up in knots and he was *tired*.

Teresa pulled in a deep breath and let it out slowly as she followed Rico. Whatever he had planned for her, it looked as though it wasn't going to happen tonight. So it seemed she was just going to have to learn to live with the jittering nerve endings and the screaming hormones. Because she wasn't about to let him know just how much his kiss had awakened in her.

He already had the power here. No point in crowning him a true King.

For the next few days, Rico was like a man holding on to a live electrical wire. His body was in a constant state of burning. He was touchy. Jumpy. And so damned horny he wondered if a man could die from *want*.

The plan had been to keep Teresa with him at all times, taking every chance to touch her. To kiss her. To make her so crazy she'd beg him to take her. Joke was on him though, as he was the one suffering.

He walked into the tropical bar, glancing around at the

crowd gathered beneath rainbow-colored umbrellas. Not far away, waves rushed to shore, leaving frothy footprints in their wake. Surfers rode the waves and tanned beauties lay stretched out under the sun on royal-blue chaises that looked like sapphires on the white sand. And here in the bar, conversations were loud, laughter was bright and liquor flowed as freely as the sea.

He scanned the faces gathered there and finally found the one he sought. Teresa was behind the bar, helping Teddy, the bartender, serve drinks. Rico wasn't sure why it irritated him to find her there, helping. But it did. Hell, she was supposed to be miserable. Instead her eyes were shining, her smile wide and welcoming, and when she laughed at something a customer said to her, everything inside Rico tightened into a fist.

Before he could go to her, though, a hand came down on his arm and he looked to his left. Serenity James, Hollywood's latest darling and Rico's current annoyance, smiled up at him.

She tossed her caramel-colored hair back from her shoulders to make sure her no doubt surgically enhanced breasts in her impossibly small bikini were displayed to their best advantage.

"Rico, I've been hoping to see you," she said, her voice a breathy promise of sex in silk sheets. "I wanted to thank you for finding my diamonds."

The diamonds she was wearing right now. Apparently in the young actress's eyes, beachwear also demanded accessories clearly worth more than half a million dollars. The stones glittered against her tanned skin and she ran one fingertip over the diamonds, as if to reassure herself they were still where they belonged.

"It was my pleasure," he said politely, though it cost

him. He flicked a glance at Teresa, still laughing with her customer. She was supposed to be suffering, he told himself. Instead, she was making herself at home on Tesoro. He'd noticed over the last few days just how often she lent a hand to one of the staff. The bar today, yesterday it had been some crisis in the kitchen and before that, he'd caught her helping one of the maids whose service cart had been upended by a drunken guest.

Teresa was ingratiating herself with everyone on the island. Including Sean and Melinda King. He knew that Melinda and Teresa had spent some time together since their shared dinner that first night. According to Sean, Teresa was wonderful, being good company and keeping Melinda from worrying about the unknown terrors of her impending labor.

She was winning hearts and minds everywhere. And she was making him just a little insane. His plan was going nowhere fast and time was slipping by. Meanwhile, he was trapped with the empty-headed actress smiling up at him as if she wanted to take a bite out of him. Perhaps at some point in his past he would have been tempted to allow her to do just that. But since meeting Teresa, no other woman interested him in the slightest.

So he gritted his teeth and focused on getting rid of Serenity James as quickly and discreetly as possible.

"As a guest at Castello Tesoro," he said, "you are my priority, Serenity. We want you to be happy and enjoy your time on the island."

"Well, that's the nicest thing anyone's said to me all day." She threaded her arm through his and steered him off to her table. "Join me for a drink so I can thank you again."

Annoyance scratched at the base of his spine, but he

kept his professional smile firmly in place. There was no way out of this and Rico knew it. He was used to playing host to the wealthy and the spoiled. And sometimes that meant temporarily burying his own wants and needs to keep the guests happy. Besides, Teresa wasn't going anywhere.

He took a seat beside the actress at her table. While Serenity told him all about her latest movie and asked him where she could find some real "action" on the island, Rico's mind wandered to the brunette behind the bar.

For three days and nights, they'd shared his home. His bedroom. His *bed.* Every night he lay beside her in the dark and called on every reserve of willpower he possessed to keep from touching her and taking what he still thought of as *his.* His mind filled with images, memories, of burying his body deep within hers. Tension coiled so hard and fast inside him it was a wonder he slept at all. But he would finally fall asleep, only to wake up with Teresa curled up against him, her arm flung across his chest, her head nestled on his shoulder. The scent of her filled his lungs and made waking both pleasure and agony.

Though she went to sleep clinging to the edge of the bed like the last leaf on a tree in autumn, by morning, Teresa was all over him.

She wasn't being tortured by his plan.

He was.

Serenity dragged the tips of her bloodred nails across the back of his hand. But rather than the seductive sensation she no doubt hoped it was, all Rico felt was irritation. He drew his hand back and gave her a smile. "If there's anything we can do to ensure your stay is a pleasant one, you must tell me."

Instantly her grass-green eyes flashed with interest and more. No, that wasn't what he'd meant, but women like Serenity saw only what they wished.

"Now that you mention it," she said on a throaty purr, "why don't you and I go to my cottage right now and have a private party? We could get to know each other better and—"

Before he could speak, he heard Teresa's voice come from directly behind him.

"A private party?" she repeated, coming around to sit on the arm of Rico's chair. She laid one arm around his shoulders and he felt her breast press against him as she leaned in.

Curious as to what she was up to, he didn't say a word to stop her.

"Shouldn't you be behind the bar mixing drinks?" Serenity asked coolly, her gaze moving up and down Teresa's outfit of cotton-candy-pink T-shirt, white shorts and flip-flops with dismissal.

"Oh," Teresa cooed, "I'm much more than a bartender, Ms. James."

Rico was enjoying himself. Teresa's hand slid back and forth across his shoulder, then moved up to the nape of his neck, where her fingers threaded through his hair with slow strokes. His skin was sizzling and every drop of blood in his body suddenly rushed south.

"Now, if you don't mind," Teresa said, giving the other woman a sweet smile, "my *husband* and I have other plans."

"Husband?" Serenity looked from Rico to Teresa and back again. "You're *married?*"

Rico bit back an oath as the actress's voice hitched high enough to be heard at the surrounding tables. His marriage had never been public knowledge. His and Teresa's time together had been so short that not even the media had caught on to it before she had disappeared from his life. Now, though, that looked as if it was about to change.

"Well, damn it," Serenity said on a full-bottom-lip pout, "you could have *mentioned* it." When she stood up in a huff, she punched her breasts out to make sure he could appreciate what he'd be missing, then turned and sashayed—the only word to describe the swing of her hips and the long stride of golden legs—out of the bar.

When she was gone, Teresa made a move to get up, but Rico caught her around the waist and dragged her down onto his lap. Her sexy, curvy behind nestled on top of him and Rico knew a whole new world of discomfort. He groaned, but held her in place. Yes, there was pain, but there was also need and want and a hunger like he hadn't known in five years. She wiggled, trying to get up, but her movements only fanned the flames licking at him.

"Let me up," she said in a whisper. "People are watching."

"You made sure of that when you walked up and rubbed yourself against me," he told her, enjoying the memory almost as much as the feel of her sitting on him.

"I didn't—" She broke off. "Fine. I did."

"Question is," he asked, "why?"

She looked down into his eyes and seemed to consider whether she would answer or not. After a long minute or two, she tore her gaze from his and muttered, "You looked like you wanted to be rescued."

"Ah." He hid a satisfied smile. He hadn't needed saving. Teresa had chased off the actress for her own reasons. Maybe his plan of seduction was actually working better than he had thought. "That's another lie. You're very good at it, by the way, but not good enough."

"Well, if I read you wrong and you *didn't* want to be saved from a conversation with that vacuous twit, I'm so very sorry."

A smile ticked up the corner of his mouth. "Twit? Have you met Ms. James before, then?"

"I don't need to talk to her to recognize the type," Teresa said, studying her fingernails now as if the secrets of the universe were scribed there.

"Which is?"

She shrugged and that little movement had her shifting on his lap again. Rico had to hiss in a breath to keep from groaning aloud. It was the sweetest kind of pain he'd ever known and he was in no hurry to ease it.

"She's pretty and has great boobs, which she probably paid a fortune for, and that's about it."

Rico smirked at her. "You can tell this with a glance?"

"Absolutely," she said. "But if you want to chase Ms. Boobs, just say so."

He shook his head. "I'm not interested in Serenity."

"Not how it looked from the bar." And she was back to studying her nails.

"You were jealous."

She stiffened in outrage and glared at him for good measure. "I don't know what you're talking about."

"Yes, you do." He dropped one hand to her thigh and relished the feel of her sun-warmed skin, bared by her white shorts.

She shivered and tried to scoot to one side, but his other arm wrapped around her waist held her exactly where he wanted her. He continued to stroke her thigh and felt the tremble shaking her slide under his own skin, as well.

Surrounded by guests enjoying the beach, Rico felt as if he and Teresa were alone. Only the two of them in this moment. And hell, it would have been much easier on him if they *had* been alone. Then he could just stretch her out on the sand, strip her clothes off and give in.

"You are lying again. To me. To yourself."

She huffed out a breath and squirmed on his lap, which only served to make him harder and her more aware of it. Instantly, she stilled. "What do you want to hear, Rico?"

"The truth," he said, in a direct challenge. "That you didn't like seeing that woman with me."

She laughed, but the sound lacked her usual musical quality and came off as strained instead. "If I were the jealous type, the last five years of seeing your picture in magazines and newspapers, always with a different woman, would have drummed that right out of me."

"So you tell yourself. And yet…"

Teresa took a breath, slanted her eyes to his and murmured, "Fine. I didn't like the way she was pawing at you. Heck, she was practically drooling. Happy now?"

Short answer was yes. A longer answer would take more time. At least a couple of hours. In his bed. Even his taste for revenge was muted by the fire inside him. All he wanted, all he could think about, was getting her naked and—if he didn't stop thinking about it he'd never be able to walk out of the bar.

Reluctantly, he relaxed his hold on her and she quickly got to her feet. She looked down at him and her eyes were bright, her mouth parted as her breath came fast and hard. He caught one of her hands in his and rubbed his thumb across her knuckles. She pulled her hand free a moment later and he allowed it.

"I'll see you back at the house," he said quietly. "One hour."

She swallowed hard and suddenly looked just a little… anxious. "Rico—"

"One hour, Teresa. Then we settle this between us."

She gave him a brief nod, then moved back to the bar. Alone, Rico stared out at the sea, trying to empty his mind of every wicked thought and desire that raced through it. What he needed was a cold shower, but what he wanted was more heat. Teresa's heat. The fire he had only ever experienced with her.

And soon he would have it.

Six

Teresa was standing on his bedroom terrace when he arrived. The tropical breeze smelled of saltwater and flowers. The sound of the ocean was like a heartbeat in the distance and the dappled shade from the surrounding trees danced and shifted with the wind that lifted her hair from her shoulders in soft waves.

Her heart was pounding. Every nerve in her body was standing straight up and buzzing. She felt electrified from the inside out. She couldn't sit still. Couldn't stand without moving, pacing. Could hardly breathe through the knot of anticipation lodged in her throat.

Back at the beach bar, when she'd been sitting on Rico's lap, she'd felt the hard proof of his desire for her. And even there, surrounded by strangers, she'd wanted nothing more than to turn in the chair, straddle him and— *Oh boy, she was in very serious trouble.*

Feeling this way for your husband was one thing. Wanting the man who only wanted to use you then discard you was simply a road map to misery. God, she remembered so clearly what it was like to be loved by Rico King. To be the reason his eyes warmed when she walked into a room. To know that he was right there if she stretched out her hand. To have his arms come around her in the middle of the night, making her feel safe and treasured.

And she knew what it was like to lose all of it.

Now she would have to lose it *again,* and Teresa didn't know if she'd be able to bear it this time. Because she'd already lived through years of emptiness without him, so this time when she left, she knew exactly the kind of cold, dark place that would be waiting for her. She'd do anything to avoid that wide chasm of utter loneliness again. But there was just no way out.

Her careening thoughts skidded to a halt when she actually *felt* Rico's presence. Slowly she turned to see him standing in the open doorway, watching her. The wind caught his hair and tossed it across his forehead. His blue eyes were fixed on her and his mouth was tight, as if he wished he were anywhere but here. And yet…there was heat and tension spiraling between them, binding them together with invisible tendrils of desire and need.

Whatever else also lay between them—lies, betrayal, anger—this was just as real. This living, breathing passion that was so strong it was pushing her to take the first steps toward him even now. It didn't matter why he wanted her. Only that he did. She couldn't take another moment without feeling his hands on her. She'd wanted for so long and now she could *have.*

He held his ground, half in the bedroom, half out, and

waited for her to come closer. Every step was a test in courage. Every breath a victory. She couldn't look away from his eyes and when she saw a flash of heat dazzling there, she crossed the last of the space separating them in a dash.

Teresa threw herself at him and he caught her, encircling her in his arms, holding her tightly to him so that she could feel every ridge and plane of his body. She felt the thick hardness of him pressed against her middle and instantly she went hot and wet.

Here, her mind whispered. *Here* was where she belonged. Where she always wanted to be.

What sounded like a growl erupted from his throat as he threaded his fingers through her hair, tipped her head back and held her for his kiss. She met him eagerly, hungrily. Their mouths fused, tongues twisting and dancing in a frenzy of need. Breathing was short and labored. Hands slid up and down burning bodies and when he suddenly turned and walked her backward toward the bed, she kept pace.

Teresa fell back onto the mattress and kept her arms around Rico's neck, as if a part of her was afraid that he would stop now. Take that one step away and return to that careful, cold distance between them just to torture her. But she wouldn't let him. Not this time.

Every night she slept beside him and every morning she woke up entangled with him, feeling the heat of his body pouring into hers just before he bolted from the bed and left her there. Alone.

She was done.

Let the revenge begin.

She didn't care *why* she was there anymore. Or even

why he wanted her there. It was enough that Rico was with her again, laying his body atop hers.

Finally he tore his mouth from hers, looked down into her eyes and whispered, "You're wearing too many clothes."

"You, too."

Nodding, he rolled to one side of her and got up just long enough to yank his clothes off and toss everything to the floor. Teresa did the same. Her T-shirt, shorts and sandals were on the floor in seconds and her bra and panties quickly followed. Then she was naked, standing in front of him as the sunlight streaming through the terrace doors caressed their already-heated bodies in a golden warmth that seemed to soak deep into their bones. That light was reflected in his eyes as he looked at her and Teresa shivered in response.

He was beautiful. Just as she remembered him. His body was tanned and every muscle was sharply defined. He was also hard and ready and glancing at his erection made Teresa quiver deep inside. Right where she wanted him.

As if reading her thoughts, Rico reached for her, then tumbled her back onto the mattress. Heated skin met the cool silk of the duvet beneath her and seemed to heighten every one of her senses to overload.

Rico's hands skimmed over her body. Her breasts, her nipples, her abdomen and finally lower, where he cupped her heat and rubbed the heel of his hand against her until she was writhing beneath him.

Her gaze still locked on his, she watched as her responses to him fed the flames dancing in those pale blue depths. She chewed at her bottom lip and a soft moan slipped from her mouth as he dipped first one finger and then two into her heat.

Teresa sighed at the blissful sensation of his touch on her body again. Everything was so familiar and yet so new. Almost as if this was their first time together. Her hands moved over his shoulders and down his arms, stroking, loving the feel of his skin beneath her hands. He was so hard and strong and so warm to the touch.

He bent his head to her breast and as she watched, he took one of her already-peaked nipples into his mouth. She gasped at the first touch of his lips and tongue. She moaned as his teeth scraped across the sensitive tip and then she arched into him as he suckled her.

His hand stroked her core while his mouth drove her even closer to the edge. Again and again, he drew on her breast, as if he could taste all she was. She felt that drawing sensation down to her bones and all she could think was, *yes. This is all just as it should be.*

This was what had tormented her dreams for so long. The memories of his touch, his caresses, his mouth, his hot breath dusting across her skin. All she needed now to feel complete was his body pushing into hers, locking them together as they were meant to be.

He lifted his head as if he'd heard or sensed her thoughts. Staring into her eyes, he whispered, "You feel so good, Teresa. As I remembered and more."

"Rico…" That single word came out strangled as knots of need lodged in her throat and breathing was more and more difficult.

Her hips lifted into his hand and his thumb brushed across one particular spot of sensation that had her reaching blindly for him. He kissed her again and again, mouths meeting and parting, breath mingling, their heavy sighs coming in tandem.

Teresa struggled to find her breath as Rico drove her toward a climax she didn't want to experience without him inside her. "Be with me, Rico. Be *in* me."

He hissed in a breath, dropped his forehead to hers for a moment and then eased up enough to look into her eyes. "No, Teresa. When I have you, it will be *my* way."

Her heart broke a little even as her body was clamoring for more. "Don't," she urged, framing his face in her hands. "Don't use what's between us for payback."

His hand on her core stilled and her body ached.

"If I wanted to torture you," he said softly, kissing her mouth, her nose, her eyes, "I would step away now and leave you hungering for me as I hungered for you so long ago."

Guilt rushed in and chewed at her heart. She had walked out on the man she loved without explanation. Without apologies. Just disappeared one day and as far as he knew, never looked back. But it hadn't been easy for her. She'd left a piece of her soul behind when she'd slipped away from his life. A piece she could never reclaim.

"Rico, I hungered, too," she whispered and felt the sting of tears in her eyes. "I didn't want to leave you. I had to—"

Sunlight shone in the black of his hair and glittered across his blue eyes. Outside the terrace doors, the surrounding trees were filled with birds screeching and singing. Inside, silence was as heavy as stone.

He shook his head. "No more. The past is gone. What we have is now. This month and no longer."

There it was. He couldn't have been clearer. From

the first time he'd proposed this blackmailed month to this very moment, Rico had laid down his expectations. One month. No longer. Her insides twisted and her heart wept, but her body was more interested in the *now*. In the completion of the orgasm that had been promised.

"This month, then," she said softly and thought that she saw, however briefly, a flicker of regret in his eyes. But in the next moment, it was gone anyway.

She smoothed one hand across his face as he touched her again, sliding his fingers deep inside her. He stroked her inside and out, increasing the rhythm of his caresses until all thought but one was chased from her mind. She needed.

All she could see was his eyes. Those blue depths that were filled with so many colliding emotions she couldn't identify them. All she felt was the tightening coil inside her, threatening to explode.

"Rico, please. Now. Be with me." She bucked against him and tossed her head from side to side. Her heartbeat clamored in her chest and it felt as though every muscle in her body was clenched. Feet planted on the mattress beneath her, she moved into his hand, seeking more, needing more.

When he stopped touching her and pulled away, she groaned tightly. "Don't stop. Please. Don't stop."

"I'm not," he said through gritted teeth. "I couldn't even if I wanted to."

She heard a drawer open and close, then the distinct sound of a foil wrapper being ripped open. She opened her eyes, looked at him in time to see him sheathe himself and her mouth went dry again. He was the most beautiful man she had ever seen. How had she ever had the courage to leave him and what she'd found with him? How would she ever survive without him again?

But those thoughts and the millions of others that would no doubt torment her for years to come had no place here now. Here there was only she and Rico. And the passion rising in the room.

Teresa lifted her arms to him and parted her legs in welcome. His body covered hers and in the next breath he entered her, sliding into her heat in one long, smooth stroke. She sighed in soul-deep pleasure at the feel of him within her once more. So long. It had been so very long.

Teresa's head tipped back on the mattress and she lifted her legs higher, wrapping them around Rico's waist, holding him to her, taking him as deeply as she could. She wanted to savor the moment. Imprint the feel of him inside her on her brain so that the sensation became a part of her. So that she would never truly feel alone again.

"Look at me," he whispered and Teresa opened her eyes to stare into his. Her own desire was reflected back at her and matched by what was shining in his gaze.

He set a rhythm that she eagerly met and as they looked into each other's eyes, they raced toward completion together. Teresa shouted his name as pleasure, raw and wild, crashed over her and as her arms locked around him, she heard him groan, felt him stiffen as his own release claimed him.

And locked together, they tumbled over the edge and willingly fell into oblivion.

A half hour later, Teresa was feeling wonderful. Sprawled across a bed, her lover—her husband—lay beside her. Every inch of her body felt well used. Her heart was full and in that moment, her mind raced with possibilities.

Maybe this month wouldn't be the end after all, she thought, refusing for now to remember Rico's words, *This month and no longer.* Maybe it could still be different. Maybe this time with him would be a beginning. A fresh start. A time for them to meet as equals and realize that what they had found together was too precious to throw away. Maybe there could still be a happily ever after.

But not, she knew, until the past had finally been put to rest.

"Rico," she said, voice soft in the quiet room, "I want you to know that when I left five years ago—"

"Stop." He cut her off with one sharp word. Turning his head to meet her eyes, he said, "I'm not interested in remembering old lies—or hearing new ones."

His cold tone was like a verbal slap. "I wasn't going to—"

"Teresa," he said on a sigh, "this changes nothing between us, so don't look at me with stars in your eyes."

God, she had been. And she should have known better. But how was she supposed to protect her heart against hope?

"I need a shower." Rico pushed off the bed, gave her a quick look and said, "That was good, thanks."

"Thanks?" Stunned, she looked up at him. "That's it? Just *thanks?*"

He shrugged. "Were you expecting outpourings of love and devotion?" He smiled briefly and shook his head. "All we share now is sex and this hotel, Teresa. And that only for the next month."

Hurt crowded around her heart and squeezed painfully. Just a short while ago, he had been a part of her, sharing something *amazing,* and now he'd draped that icy demeanor over himself like a damn cloak. There was distance in his voice and a careless attitude that tore at the last remaining shreds of five-year-old dreams.

"That wasn't just *sex,* Rico." There was more between them than that. Wasn't there?

He met her gaze thoughtfully for a long second or two. Then he said simply, "Yes, it was."

Turning his back on her, he stalked toward the spa-like bathroom and tossed over his shoulder, "You should get cleaned up. We're expected for dinner at Sean and Melinda's."

Then he closed the bathroom door behind him and left her, suddenly cold and very much alone, in the middle of the bed.

Dinner was an eternity.

Pretending as if nothing was wrong only built the tension inside Rico until he felt as though he would *snap*. He'd finally escaped to the patio of Sean's home, where he stood alone in the starry darkness. Solar lights made circles of gold on the neatly tended lawn. Mature trees surrounded the house and yard and a stone walkway led down to the ocean.

He listened now, letting the soothing charge and retreat of the surf sink into him, hoping to relax some before rejoining the others inside. It wasn't easy to act as though all was well. It went against his nature to be less than honest. He was uncomfortable with pretense. Lies were tangled webs, snaring everyone who came close. And the lies Teresa had told so long ago were still strangling him.

Rico had never been one to accept lies. When he was a boy, his mother had concocted stories with impunity to get whatever she wanted. He'd never been able to believe a word she said because lying had become second nature to her. When Rico was eleven, she had at last given him up to be raised by his father, Mike King. He remembered his father coming to him several months later, asking him if he missed his mother. The sad truth was, he hadn't missed her at all, because he'd never really known her.

Her lies and impossible-to-believe stories had ensured that she was a mystery, even to her son. When she died ten years ago, she had still been a nebulous figure to Rico. He had no idea who she had been. What she'd believed. If she'd loved him at all. The lies had clouded everything.

Truth was much cleaner. Much more…efficient.

But lies kept entangling him.

For example, the lie he'd told himself: that having Teresa back in his bed would rid him of the remains of his desire for her. Instead he wanted her now more than ever.

And that shook him.

Then there was the lie he had told Teresa: that it had been simply sex that they'd shared. It cost Rico to admit it, but he couldn't hide the truth from himself. What he'd just experienced with Teresa was something else again. His whole damn body felt as if it were burning up from the inside. The tension that had been clawing at him since he'd first seen Teresa here on the island was as raw and fresh as ever. He felt as tightly wound as he ever had and he knew that his revenge plan had suddenly turned on him.

He turned away from the garden view and looked at the well-lit house behind him. Through the wide bay window in the huge kitchen, he could see Teresa with Melinda, and the two women seemed to be having a good time. No one would guess that only a couple of hours ago, Teresa had been wild in his arms. Or that he'd seen hurt in her eyes when he'd dismissed what they'd shared.

But he knew, and the memories were choking him.

"Plan not going so well?"

Rico glanced at Sean as his cousin walked out to join him on the patio. "What makes you say that?"

"For starters, you're strangling that poor, innocent beer bottle."

Rico cursed under his breath and carefully eased his grip on the bottle neck. "I've a lot on my mind."

"Yeah." Sean looked over his shoulder at the two women standing in the home King Construction had built for his family. "It's pretty clear just what's on your mind."

"Stay out of this, Sean." Even Rico heard his accent thicken as his voice dropped to a dangerous tone. He'd spent most of his early youth in Mexico with his mother. Much later he had gone to California to live with his father's family. And still, at emotional or stressful times, the music of an accent appeared in his speech.

Sean lifted both hands in false surrender. "Hey, I'm out. What you do to screw up your world is your business."

Annoyance flared and Rico scowled at the other man. He loved his family—all of them. But he knew their flaws and the worst one was that in the King family, even when they were "butting out," they had their say. You never had to wonder what your brothers or cousins were thinking, because there hadn't been a King born yet who could keep his opinion to himself. Every last one of them was sure he was right and didn't care who knew it. Made for some interesting family get-togethers and some very loud discussions.

Scowling, Rico took a sip of beer that he didn't want

and willed the icy brew to cool off the fires within. It didn't help any. "How's Melinda feeling?"

"Oh, nice change of subject. Very subtle." Sean snorted and leaned one hip on the patio railing. His gaze still focused on his wife through the wide bay window, he sighed. "She's nesting. I swear, Rico, the more nervous I get, the more *serene* she gets."

"Probably in self-defense," Rico mused. "Watching you go crazy with worry, she can either go with you or…"

"Yeah." Sean scraped one hand over his face. "Okay, yeah, I am going a little nuts. But damn, Rico. I'm about to be a *father*. That's just scary as hell."

"It must be." For one incredibly brief instant, Rico's mind dredged up an image of Teresa, pregnant with his child. Then that image shattered and he mentally swept up the shards and disposed of them.

"I mean," Sean was saying, "what the hell do I know about being a father? What if I mess it up?"

"You won't."

"Yeah? My dad wasn't the best role model in the world."

True. Sean's father, Ben King, had many sons and had never married any of their mothers. He had done his best by his children, but he hadn't always been around for them. Rico could understand Sean's doubts even as he knew that Sean would never let down his children or his wife.

"You're better than that."

"I'd like to think so," Sean admitted, then he gave a shaky laugh. "But the God's truth is, this is…huge. My kids will be looking to *me* for answers, about life and the world and—" He shook his head and took a long pull of his beer. "Okay, freaking out a little, I guess."

"It's understandable." Rico slapped his cousin on the back. "But some of your brothers are fathers. Surely they can give you some tips."

Sean laughed a little and shook his head. "Yeah, if you listen to Lucas, his Danny is ready for college and the kid's just about to turn three. And as for Rafe, his and Katie's daughter, Becca, is only a few months old. He's still as confused as I feel."

Chuckling in spite of everything, Rico reminded him, "In the last few years, how many of our brothers and cousins have begun multiplying? Think about it, Sean. If they can handle being fathers, so can you."

"How do I know *they're* doing it right?" Sighing, he admitted, "Nope, there's no hope for this kid. I'm all he's got and I don't know what the hell I'm doing."

All joking aside, Sean really did look as though he was worried about this, so Rico took pity on his cousin.

"You will love your son, Sean. That's all he really needs from you."

"Well, that much I can do for sure," Sean said with a nervous grin. Shaking his head again, he admitted, "You know, nothing in my life has ever made me so happy and at the same time scared me boneless as the idea of my son being born."

"I think," Rico told him, "that is how it is supposed to be." He used his beer to point at the kitchen window. "Besides, look at your lovely wife. Does she look worried? No. Because she has you. And because she knows that the two of you are making a family."

Sean blew out a breath. "When did you get so damn smart?"

Rico laughed at the idea. *Smart.* If he was smart, he wouldn't have wedged himself into his current situation with Teresa. "It's not being smart," he said. "It is knowing my family. And you will be a good father, Sean."

"Hope you're right." He grinned. "No backing out now. Hey, did I tell you Melinda and I are taking the baby to California for Christmas? Get a chance to let everyone meet our new son and I can show her around Long Beach…"

Rico was only half listening now. His focus was Teresa. She was wearing a short-sleeved green silk blouse and a pair of white slacks and she looked…edible. His insides twisted anew as fresh desire pulsed in his bloodstream. She smiled and tossed her hair back from her face. The line of her throat was elegant. The shine in her eyes was magnetic. Her lush body was everything a man dreamed of.

"Oh, yeah," Sean said on a laugh, catching Rico's attention. "Your plan's working real well. Damn, dude. You can help me, but you can't dig yourself out of your own mess."

Rico straightened up. He ignored Sean's teasing and snapped out, "Melinda."

Behind the glass, Sean's wife had doubled over, one arm wrapped around her belly. Teresa was hovering over her and throwing a frantic look to Rico.

"Holy—" Sean broke off and ran. "It's time. Get the car."

Seven

In fifteen minutes, the four of them were at the hospital and Melinda and Sean were taken away to the mysteries of the maternity ward.

Then time started ticking past so slowly that Teresa almost thought they'd stepped into some vortex where time had actually stopped.

The waiting room was long and narrow. It had mint-green paint, beige linoleum floors and the most uncomfortable chairs she had ever experienced. And why, she asked herself, did all hospitals smell the same? In America, Italy, even here on this beautiful tropical island, hospitals stank of antibacterial cleansers and fear. She wrapped her arms around herself, stood up and walked out to the light-filled hallway. Across from her was a nurses' station, manned by one very tired-looking woman. Teresa didn't bother to ask any questions, mainly because Rico had been plaguing the poor woman for hours now and Teresa just didn't have the heart to bother her more.

During the long night, anxious husbands and excited grandparents had come and gone from this waiting room, and still she and Rico waited. Teresa took a seat in the narrow, nearly empty lobby, ignored the small television on the wall playing an old movie she had no interest in and stared instead at Rico, who hadn't stopped pacing since they arrived. She could understand that.

She'd realized from the moment she met him that as a King, he didn't accept inactivity easily. He was a man who took charge. Who stepped in to do what needed doing. It was part of his nature. His heritage. And now he was in the position of being able to do *nothing*.

Helplessness was not something he was even remotely familiar with.

"You might as well sit down," she finally said. "This could take a long time."

"It has already been *hours*." Frowning, he glanced at her, then fired a hard look at a passing nurse. "How much longer? And how can we know if no one will tell us anything?"

Teresa took a chance and threaded her arm through his. When he didn't shrug her off, she called it a win and smiled to herself. "Let's take a walk."

"What?" He looked down at her. "Where? I don't want to go far—what if…?"

"We won't be far," Teresa said, touched that he cared for his family this much. It was these few moments, when he was unguarded, that allowed her a glimpse of the man she'd met so long ago. This man was the Rico she remembered. The stranger was the man who had jumped out of bed as if it were on fire.

"Didn't you tell Sean that nowhere on this island was far from anything?"

"Good point." He blew out a breath and scraped one hand through his hair. "All right, then. I could use some fresh air."

"And I think the nurses could use a break, too." Teresa patted his arm as they walked past the nurses' station. She paused there only long enough to say, "We're going outside for a few minutes. If Sean comes out looking for us, tell him we'll be right back."

"I will." Her gaze fixed on Rico, she said, "You take your time."

Teresa laughed, but Rico's expression didn't change in the slightest. He still wore a frown that would send most people scrambling for a place to hide. Shaking her head, Teresa led him to the elevator, then punched the button for the main floor. The two-story building wasn't large, but it spread out over quite an area. It was the only medical facility for the islanders. Without it, people who needed serious medical help would have had to board a boat for St. Thomas.

She'd learned a lot in the last few days. Rico's employees were eager to talk about him and the island paradise where they lived. They had told her all about what the Kings had done for Tesoro since moving here. For example, they had donated enough money to see to it that the small hospital now boasted top-of-the-line, state-of-the-art equipment. They'd hired more doctors and nurses and made it possible for most emergencies to be handled on island.

They'd rebuilt the dock and improved the harbor, making it easier for charter ships, as well as local fishermen, to pull into port. In town they'd arranged for more of

the islanders to sell their wares to the tourists who now
flocked to Tesoro. The Kings had done good things on
the island and everyone here seemed to appreciate it. But
Teresa knew that if she commented on any of this to Rico,
he would shrug off her admiration and call it simply good
business. He was a complicated man and maybe that was
one reason she was so drawn to him. Because at the heart
of it, very few men were complicated.

At the ground floor, Rico practically lunged off the
elevator and Teresa had to hurry to keep up with him.
Outside the night was quiet, the wind was soft and the
sound of the ocean rumbled in the distance. It felt good
to get out of the claustrophobic waiting room. It felt even
better to have Rico beside her.

Teresa took a long, deep breath and blew it out again.
"Nice to get out of the hospital for a while."

"Yes." Rico looked back over his shoulder at the
brightly lit entrance. "But not for too long. I want to be
nearby when—"

"We will be." Teresa took his hand and was pleased
when he didn't pull away. Small victories. She led him
across the side yard, their steps muffled by the thick
grass. "But waiting for hours can be hard. You have to
get out now and then."

He snorted, but the tension in him eased a bit as the
trade winds continued to rush past them, carrying the
scents of flowers and the sea with them. "And how do
you know so much about women in childbirth?"

Teresa smiled and squeezed his hand. Whatever else
was between them, for the moment they were on the same
side, allies against the unknown.

"I grew up all over the world," she said finally, tipping

her head back to look up at the night sky, dazzled with stars. "Our home was in Italy, but we were rarely there."

"I wondered why I have more of an accent than you do."

She shrugged as if it didn't matter, when the truth was all of her life she had longed for a place to call home. Even her own apartment in Naples wasn't home. Just another temporary refuge.

"Hard to adopt a particular accent when you're never in one place long enough to pick up the rhythms of the local speech."

"Hmm…"

His noncommittal answer told her that he was thinking about the Coretti family and their tradition of thievery keeping them on the move. But she wasn't going to talk about her family now and ruin this momentary truce.

"Anyway, we were living in New York and my mother's sister was having a baby. I was about sixteen, I guess."

"And you waited as we are now?"

"We waited. For hours." She sighed and shifted her gaze from the skies to him. "It seemed to take forever."

"And did your father fill his time by stealing from the patients and doctors?"

She stopped dead and turned to face him. Her gaze met his and she was sorry to see the stony glint in his eyes again. "Can you never let it go, Rico? Not even for a while?"

"Why should I?" he demanded.

"Because I'm not my father." Her voice was quiet but strong. Her gaze never left his as she added, "I've never stolen anything in my life. I'm not a thief."

A muscle twitched in his jaw as if he were fighting an

internal battle over what to say and what to hold back. Then he blurted, "So just a liar, then?"

The verbal slap hit home and she winced. It seemed that their momentary truce had ended and her sorrow was quickly swallowed by impatience. He was determined to see her only as treacherous and Teresa had no idea how to change his mind.

"And you've never lied? Are you that perfect, Rico?"

"Not perfect," he countered. "But I don't lie to the people who matter to me."

"Ah," she said, crossing her arms over her chest and giving him a sharp nod. "So you're a picky liar. Only a select few. I'm guessing women?"

"Mostly," he admitted and didn't look bothered by the admission at all.

"And that's okay?"

"I didn't say that."

"You didn't have to." She shook her head and asked, "What about me? Did you tell me pretty lies when we met?"

His jaw clenched and it looked as though he were grinding his teeth into powder. "You're the one who lied to me, remember?"

"So you were honest with me, but not with other women." She laughed shortly. "Well, hell, Rico. You're wasting your time being a hotelier when you should be a saint."

Furious now, she let her temper reign because that was so much easier than dealing with the disappointment and regret threatening to choke her. Teresa spun around and took two steps away from him before he caught her with one strong hand and whipped her back around to face him.

"I never claimed to be a saint," he muttered, his accent suddenly flaring into life and coloring his words with a seductive tang he probably didn't intend at the moment. "But I never lied to *you*."

"What about the phony divorce papers?"

He frowned, gritted his teeth and kept quiet, silently admitting he had no answer for that.

Taking a deep breath, she looked up into his eyes and searched for the man she loved behind that wall of ice he'd built between them. "I didn't want to lie to you, Rico. I didn't want to leave you, either. But there was nothing else I could do. Can't you understand lying to protect someone?"

"I can't understand a family who demands that kind of loyalty."

"Really?" She tipped her head to one side and met him, glare for glare. "Because the King family isn't loyal?"

"We don't cheat for each other," he snapped. "We don't lie to protect each other."

"But you would if you had to."

His mouth flattened into a grim slash and his eyes narrowed. She could see that he was thinking about it, considering…and not really enjoying the answer he was coming up with.

She took a long breath. "Rico, I'm not asking you to forget what happened five years ago. But maybe you could try to see it from my side."

"Your side? All I know of your side is one thing." He released his hold on her, shoved his hands into his pockets and stared over her head at the surrounding trees. "You chose them over me."

"They're my family."

His gaze shot to hers. "And I'm your *husband*."

"Do you really think it was easy for me?"

"All I know is that you did it," he ground out. "Easy or difficult, you made your choice and we were both forced to live with it."

Pain squeezed her heart and radiated out to every square inch of her body. There was nothing she could say to that. No excuse. No plea for understanding. Rico would never see what she had done as anything less than betrayal.

Their gazes locked, unspoken tension practically humming between them in the soft island air. The ocean was a murmur of sound and somewhere in the distance an animal's screech sounded out.

There was so much to say and so little all at the same time. Teresa had hoped that they might find a way to reach each other again, but for every step forward she took, Rico moved that much farther away. He was slipping away from her even as she stood beside him. Missing the feel of his touch, Teresa scrubbed her palms up and down her arms in a futile attempt to ease the chill of the cold that was deep inside her.

"Teresa," he asked quietly a moment later, "what happened?"

"What?" She shook her head and looked at him in confusion.

"With your aunt," he said, reminding her of the story she had been telling. "What happened?"

It took her a second, but a smile curved her mouth as she looked at him. Nothing had been solved. They were still on opposite sides of the same battle. But his question told Teresa that Rico, too, missed their all-too-brief truce. So she willingly played along and dipped back into her memories.

"After what seemed like forever, she had a baby boy. I saw him when he was just a few minutes old." Her smile brightened. "Luca was so tiny. And he looked just furious at the indignity of being born."

Rico smiled with her and for one long moment, it was almost as if they were…united. And it was so good Teresa didn't want that moment to end, though she knew it would. For whatever reason, Rico had decided to put their argument aside and go back to their earlier, almost friendly position. She was more than willing.

"Then I will try to be patient as we wait for the newest King to make his arrival."

"They know it's a boy?"

"They do," he said, nodding. "Just last month I helped Sean paint the baby's room."

"Melinda showed me the nursery. You guys did a nice job. I love the blue and chocolate-brown." She stopped and laughed a little. "Wow. I just realized it was only a few hours ago that we were at Melinda's house and it feels like days."

He nodded, looked past her at the hospital entrance and said, "The waiting takes a toll."

"It does." She followed his gaze and said, "We should really get back."

"Yes. We should." He looked as reluctant to end this alone time as she felt and Teresa told herself not to make more of it than there was. Still, a tiny nugget of hope settled into a corner of her heart and wouldn't be budged.

He took her hand in his and the warmth of his skin washed through her. She held that feeling to her and told herself to remember. To etch that sensation into her heart and mind so that one day soon, when he was far out of reach, she'd be able to take out this memory and relive the feel of her hand in his.

When he led her back to the hospital, they were silent, even their footsteps muffled on the grass.

By dawn, their wait was over.

Sean strutted down the long hallway to the waiting room and greeted them both with a wide grin stretched across his face.

"Melinda's great and so is our son." He slapped his hands together and scrubbed his palms before shoving both hands through his hair. "It was—Melinda was— *amazing.*"

Rico bolted out of his chair, crossed the room and gave his cousin a brief, hard hug before stepping back and slapping Sean on the shoulder. "Congratulations! You're a father!"

"Terrifying, man," Sean told him with a shudder. "I won't lie."

Teresa winced a little at that word, half expecting a knowing glare from Rico. She was surprised, and pleased, when it didn't come. She walked to Sean and gave him a hug. "Do we get to see him?"

"Absolutely." Sean grinned at both of them again. "I came to get you so you can admire and stare with awe at the newest King."

Rico took Teresa's hand again as they followed Sean along the corridor and she had the feeling he hadn't even noticed doing it. The move had just come naturally. As if he'd needed to be linked with her for the occasion. That nugget of hope grew just a bit in spite of the fact that she tried hard to prevent it.

The hospital was small, so it didn't take long to get to the nursery. There were only three newborns nestled into clear bassinets. And only one of those three was a boy. While Sean stared at his son with the bemused expression of someone who had survived a battle when he hadn't expected to, Teresa just looked at the baby. He was perfect. Tiny and pink-cheeked and so beautiful she felt a knot of envy lodge in her throat.

"He's a good-looking baby, Sean," Rico said softly and his hand tightened imperceptibly on Teresa's.

"Yeah." Sean rocked on his heels and finally tore his gaze from his son. "He really is. You want to go see Melinda?"

They did and once in the private hospital room, Teresa and Rico stood on either side of the new mother's bed.

"He's beautiful," Teresa said.

"I know!" Melinda smiled and sighed, then unnecessarily smoothed the blanket and sheet covering her. "I can't believe he's finally here."

"What's his name?" Teresa asked, looking from one new parent to the other.

"Stryker," Sean announced with a secretive smile for his wife.

"It was my father's name," Melinda added, beaming at Sean. "My grandfather was really pleased when we told him what we were going to name the baby. And it means a lot to me, too."

"It's a big name for such a little guy," Sean mused.

"I think he will grow into it," Rico told him, with another slap on the shoulder. "Stryker King. It sounds strong."

"Yeah." Sean had a silly grin on his face. "It does."

Teresa watched Rico and his family and wished that she really belonged in that circle of familiarity. But she was a temporary blip on the King family radar. She wouldn't be here to watch Stryker grow up. She wouldn't be here to build on the friendship she and Melinda had begun. In less than a month, she would be gone and the island would go on without her. As would Rico.

She took a breath and held it. To distract herself, she glanced around. The private room was a pale yellow and a single bedside light glowed, throwing soft shadows across Melinda's features. She looked tired, but more happy than Teresa could have imagined.

Melinda grinned up at them and reached for Rico's hand. "I'm so glad you guys stayed. But you must be exhausted."

"You're the one who did all the work," Teresa pointed out.

"Hey, I was here too, you know," Sean chimed in.

His wife gave him a smile usually reserved for heroes. "You were, sweetie, and you were great." Then she sighed and leaned back into her pillow. "I am tired, but I'm so wired right now there's no way I could sleep, you know?"

"Well, if you are not tired, I'm willing to bet that you are at least hungry," Rico said.

"Oh, God." Melinda laughed. "I'm so hungry if I had any chocolate syrup to drown them in, I'd eat the sheets right off the bed."

Teresa laughed.

"But the nurse tells me that breakfast isn't served for another couple of hours…" She glanced at her husband. "I'm going to get Sean to go home and bring me a nutrition bar. Or a bag of cookies. Or both."

"I think we can do better than that." Rico leaned over the metal bed rail and kissed Melinda's forehead. Then he straightened and looked at Sean. "I will have our chef prepare something and it will be here within a half an hour."

"Oh, boy! You are a god among men, Rico," Melinda said on a sigh of gratitude.

"That has been said," he allowed.

"That's breakfast for *two,* right?" Sean put in hopefully.

"Of course."

"Feel better already." Sean grinned. "Of course, making himself the hero here, there'll be no living with him now. Good luck to you, Teresa."

A strained silence erupted suddenly as everyone in the room remembered at once that Teresa was on Tesoro only temporarily. Taking a breath, she swallowed hard and said, "Congratulations again, Melinda. Your baby is gorgeous."

"Thanks." She took Teresa's hand and held it for a second or two, offering silent support. "Once I get out of here, come to the house. I'll tell you all of my horror stories."

"Can't wait." Teresa smiled, then walked around the end of the bed to join Rico.

"We will see you soon." Rico lifted one hand to Sean and slipped out the door, drawing Teresa with him.

As they walked down the hall and passed the nurses' station for the last time, Teresa said, "That was nice of you. Sending them breakfast, I mean."

"It is a small enough thing to do." He tried to shrug it off and hit the elevator button for the ground floor. In moments the doors had opened again and they were striding out of the hospital into the cool of early morning.

"You really don't like being told you're nice, do you?" She studied his profile.

"Only because I'm not. And you would have said the same yesterday."

Her steps faltered a bit, but she caught herself and hurried on. True, after he'd climbed out of bed the day before and looked at her with ice in his eyes, she wouldn't have called him nice. But he had a heart, she knew he did. She'd just seen evidence of it. And five years ago he had offered that heart to her.

Was she solely to blame for the changes in Rico? And if so, how could she undo it?

Once they were in his car and buckled up, she asked, "How will Sean get home? We brought him here."

"I'll have someone bring his car to the hospital for him."

Teresa smiled. "Nice again."

He blew out a breath and glanced at her. "Expedient."

"You can't convince me, Rico." She shook her head and relaxed back against her seat, giving in to the fatigue that had suddenly begun to drag at her. "You're a nice guy and that's not a bad thing."

"Don't make me what I'm not, Teresa," he warned and fired up the engine. "It won't serve either of us."

Sunrise streaked the sky with soft colors that grew bolder nearer the horizon. The ever-present wind sighed through the opened car windows.

She understood what Rico was trying to tell her. But in the soft light of the breaking dawn, she looked at him and saw him for *exactly* what he was.

The love of her life.

Eight

A week later, Rico stood in his office at the hotel, staring out the window at the sprawling view beyond the glass. From here he could see most of the village, the harbor and all the way to the horizon. He wasn't noticing the inherent beauty of the view at the moment though. Instead, he was trying to focus on the myriad problems facing him.

Running a luxury resort such as Castello Tesoro meant that there were small crises in the making at all times. Usually he accepted them as simply a part of his world. But with Teresa back in his life, he was less focused and so, less prepared to handle it all.

In the last few days, he had already dealt with a small fire caused by a candle left burning in one of the bungalows. No injuries, thank God, but a chaise and several throw pillows were toast. Then there was the tourist who broke an ankle jumping from the top of a waterfall on the property. He was in pain but he was lucky he hadn't broken his neck instead. Naturally, the hotel would pay for his hospital bills and Rico was arranging for private transport back to the States.

There were the small, everyday problems, as well: sunburns, jellyfish stings, drunks and the occasional brawls between guests. It was the sort of thing you expected to deal with as a hotelier. What you *didn't* normally come up against was an executive chef with appendicitis.

Rico turned his back on the window and faced his general manager, standing on the opposite side of his desk. "How long will Louis be out of commission?"

"According to the doctor, at least a week." Janine Julien, a woman of about sixty with the organizational skills of a general, tapped her computer tablet. Janine had been with him since Cancún. She'd chosen to leave her home in Mexico for the island of Tesoro and Rico had been pleased by the decision. The woman kept her finger on the pulse of the hotel and was often able to anticipate and prevent problems before they happened.

"Louis will be fine," she added. "But with him out of commission for a while, I'm more concerned about what's going to happen here. As you know, the hotel is booked solid for the foreseeable future. There's a wedding scheduled this weekend and I can't stress enough how much time Louis spent with the bride's mother going over the selected menu. She is *not* going to be happy."

"We have other chefs." Rico shrugged. "They are more than capable."

"Sure they are," Janine agreed. "But Louis keeps the kitchen running. He's more than a chef. He's the one voice amid the chaos that people listen to. We've got a problem, Rico."

He had more than one, he told himself grimly. But at the moment, straightening out the mess in the hotel kitchen took precedence over Teresa.

"And I think I've found the solution."

"What?" Rico came around his desk and perched on the front edge. Folding his arms over his chest, he asked, "A solution already?"

The woman met his gaze and said, "Your wife."

Since she had been here on the island, Teresa had become known to everyone. If they'd been surprised to discover he was married, no one had mentioned it. Rico only hoped they were as discreet when the marriage was over and Teresa was gone from the island and his life.

That thought made him frown, so he pushed it aside and turned his focus back to the older woman.

"What about Teresa?"

"She was in the kitchen helping the staff prepare when Louis collapsed." Shaking her head, Janine said, "I happened to be there, too, to discuss the individual cakes for the upcoming wedding. I saw how she took charge." Shaking her head, she continued, "I was flustered, I'll admit it. But Teresa? She checked on Louis, had someone call the hotel doctor, then had another chef drive him to the hospital. And while all of this was going on, she got the kitchen moving again."

Janine shook her head, still clearly impressed with what she'd witnessed. "Everyone was shaken, but Teresa just stepped up and took charge. No one questioned her. They got back to work, and in spite of what had happened to Louis, the staff never missed a step. She's still down there now, running things. I thought you should know."

Rico didn't know whether to be grateful or furious. Once again Teresa had proven herself to him and to his staff. She wasn't cowering in his room, as a proper hostage should be. Instead, she was making herself a part of the fabric of Castello Tesoro. He knew, too, that the fabric would unravel once she was gone.

And she would be gone.

He couldn't risk believing in her again. Couldn't take the chance of keeping her here with him, knowing that her thieving family might show up at any time. But that wasn't the truth at all. He didn't give a damn about Teresa's family and knew he could handle them if they ever showed up on Tesoro again.

This was about *her*. The woman he'd once married. The woman he had trusted. Believed in. Only to be betrayed.

Well, if she was trying to ingratiate herself with him now, it wouldn't work. Of course he'd allow her to help; he wasn't an idiot and a talented chef didn't fall out of the sky when needed. But her help was all he was interested in.

Pushing up from the desk, he barked out orders. "Contact the hospital. Take care of Louis's bill and get him whatever he wants. I'll go see him later."

"Right." Her gaze tracked him as he stalked across the room toward the office door. "Where are you going?"

"To the kitchen." He glanced over his shoulder at her. "I'll see for myself if Teresa is working out as head chef or not."

A few minutes later Rico stood in a doorway, watching the choreographed confusion in the gigantic kitchen and couldn't help but be impressed. The first thing he noticed was that the classical music Louis insisted on piping through the room had been replaced by rock, with a beat that kept the entire staff moving from station to station at a busy pace. The pastry chefs worked at a mound of dough, the salads were being prepared at a long marble counter and the prep chefs were busily preparing tonight's soup selections, as well as setting up the ingredients for the rest of the menu.

And in the middle of the chaos stood Teresa. Her black hair was pulled back and tucked up under a chef's hat. She wore a white coat over her street clothes and directed traffic in the big room like a traffic cop at a particularly busy corner.

She paused to take a sip of a sauce, then directed the chef to add something else. She inspected the pastry chefs' work and grinned at them in approval. Someone shouted a question and before they'd finished speaking, she was there, lending a hand.

Rico shook his head as he watched her. Sunlight poured in from the skylights in the roof and that golden light seemed to follow Teresa wherever she went. She shone, plain and simple. He was impressed. He didn't want to be, but there it was. Teresa had stepped in when she was most needed and was taking charge of what could have been a disastrous situation.

Everyone knew that the chefs in any big kitchen had rivalries and jealousies driving them. Without Teresa, there would have been a power play with several of the chefs making a bid to step into Louis's position. With her, the kitchen was running as well as or better than it had before.

Frowning to himself, he had to admit that there was much more to this woman than he had long believed. She wasn't here of her own free will. He had practically kidnapped her, blackmailed her, holding the freedom of her family over her head. Yet instead of standing by and watching disaster strike his hotel, she had jumped in, unasked, to save the day. Why? He had to wonder.

Unnoticed, he watched her and as he did, something within him stirred. Not the heat of desire that was a continuous, overwhelming pulse tearing through him. This was something else. There was warmth beneath the heat and a rush of feelings that he'd been denying for five long years.

As soon as he sensed that warmth settling around his heart, he bit off an oath and walked away.

It had been great to be back in a big kitchen.

Teresa had told Melinda that she'd spent the last five years working in a series of different restaurants around the world. And it was true. But they were small places— mom-and-pop diners, coffee shops and bakeries. She'd worked in a patisserie in Paris, a bakery in Gstaad and a pretzel shop in Berlin. She'd spent time in Italian restaurants in Florence and tea shops in London.

But not since she left Rico in Mexico had she worked for a five-star restaurant. Truthfully, when she had first disappeared from his hotel in Mexico, Teresa had worried that he would track her down and find her, so she'd hidden away in small eateries that most people overlooked. But after some time, she had simply gravitated to those places as if she were punishing herself by refusing the opportunity to do what she did best—run a big kitchen.

But today that had changed. She felt terrible that Louis had taken ill, but she also had to admit that she had loved the challenge of stepping into his shoes, however temporarily. She'd worked tirelessly for hours and when the guests had all been served and the ovens shut down, she'd stayed late to supervise the massive cleanup required.

By the time she was ready to go back to Rico's house and her gilded cage, Teresa was exhausted. And felt better than she had in far too long. She let herself in through the front door and quietly shut it behind her. A smile was still on her face as she headed down the long, slate-tiled hallway toward Rico's bedroom. As she passed the shadow-filled living room, his voice stopped her.

"Why did you do it?"

"Rico?" The room was dark, save for the pale, watery light spilling in from the night beyond the wide windows. "Why are you sitting down here in the dark?"

She heard a click and instantly, a fire blossomed to life in the gas hearth. Multicolored slate tiles in shades of blues and grays made up the fireplace insert. Leaping flames and fiery light jumped around the room, highlighting the man who stood before it. "I want to know why you helped out in the kitchen, Teresa. You didn't have to. It wasn't up to you to prevent a disaster."

She walked into the room, hardly noticing the brightly patterned throw rugs scattered over the floor. She paid no attention to the oversize brown leather couches and chairs or to the gleaming oak tables between them. She barely glanced through the wide window providing a spectacular view of his yard that swept down to an ocean that frothed with phosphorescent light.

"I wanted to help."

"I know that. What I don't know," he repeated, "what I need to know, is *why?*"

"Is it really so hard to understand, Rico?" she asked, walking close enough to him to stare up into eyes that were shadowed in the low light, yet danced with the re-flections of the flames.

"Yes," he whispered, gaze locked on her, moving over her features as if he'd never seen her before. "You had no reason to. I forced you to stay here on the island when you had no wish to. I've threatened your family with imprisonment and have made you a hostage. So yes, it is hard for me to understand why you would step in during a crisis at my hotel."

Teresa shook her head sadly. He couldn't see how much she loved him. Or if he did, he chose to not recognize it. So how could she explain that for her, there hadn't been a choice at all? "I wanted to help *you*, Rico. Louis got sick and I was right there, so I helped."

"What are you trying to do to me?" His voice was low, deep and rough. As if every word had to scratch its way past his throat.

"Do to you?" She huffed an impatient breath. "Nothing, Rico. I'm here for a month. Would it be easier on you if I sat in a corner and cried over being trapped here by a man who clearly can't stand to be around me unless I'm in his bed?"

"Maybe," he muttered thickly as he shoved one hand through his hair. "I don't know anymore."

Teresa didn't even know what she was feeling now. Impatience, irritation, a swell of love that was so rich and deep it filled her entire body and throbbed in her heart.

"Rico, would you rather I just sit on your bed naked, awaiting your pleasure? Would that be hostage-like enough for you?"

"Yes. No. *Yes*," he ground out, then continued in a ragged voice, "if you behaved as if you were frightened or worried, that would make more sense to me. Instead you make yourself a part of things here, even knowing you won't be staying."

"If it would help, I could whimper for a while."

He snorted. "You wouldn't know the first thing about whimpering."

A small smile curved her mouth. "At least you know me that well."

All trace of amusement drained from his features and his eyes flashed in the firelight. "Once I thought I knew you better than anyone I have ever known."

Her heart ached at the wistful tone in his voice. How much she had destroyed when she'd left. How much she'd given up, never to find again. How much they had both missed in the last five years because of a twist of fate. If Gianni hadn't stolen that dagger... If she had told Rico the truth about her family when she first met him...

But *if*s were nebulous creatures and changed nothing.

"You did know me, Rico."

"No." He shook his head and reached for her, dropping his hands onto her shoulders and pulling her up close. "I thought I did, but you weren't real. You weren't mine."

"I was, though," she argued, *willing* him to believe it.

"Not then," he answered. "Your heart was torn, your loyalties tested too deeply for you to have been mine alone. But tonight, you *are* mine."

He was right. In spite of her love for him, she *had* been torn between Rico and her family. Maybe she'd been too young to appreciate what she had found with him. She only knew that if faced with the same decision today, she would do it all differently. She would tell Rico everything and trust him to do the right thing.

God, she'd been an idiot.

She was in love with her husband and that was the one thing she could never tell him.

Rico had been waiting for her for hours. Convinced that she had an ulterior motive for offering her help when it was most needed, he'd worked it over and over again in his mind and still was no closer to discovering what her plan might be. She had to know that he hadn't changed his mind. That no matter how much she integrated herself into life on the island, he would still watch her leave at the end of the month.

She'd become friends with his cousin and his wife. The hotel staff was in love with her and he couldn't even walk into his own damned home without catching her scent. The memory of her laugh. The hush of her sighs.

When she left, it would tear a gaping hole in his life, but she *would* leave. That was their bargain and he would hold up his end. He would give her the divorce she had paid for five years ago and he would never again trust his heart to a woman.

Because even now she was keeping something from him. He didn't know what, but it was easy to read in her golden-brown eyes that she was deliberately *not* telling him everything. What her secret might be this time, he had no idea. And it bothered him more than he wanted to admit that she was *still* hiding things from him.

But through the frustration and the irritation, one thing continuously rang true. He hungered for her. He wanted her now more than ever. And the whole time he'd been here, in the dark, waiting for her, his mind had devised all manner of things he wanted to do with her when she returned. Now that she was here, in front of him, smelling so good, he drew in breath after breath just to taste her scent…Rico didn't want to wait even the length of time it would take to get to the bedroom.

"You're driving me insane, Teresa." His hand cupped her cheek, then slid around to the back of her head.

"You're not alone in that," she told him and went up on her toes.

He kissed her, hard, taking her mouth in a rush of desire and all-encompassing need. She tangled her tongue with his, leaning into him for support and wrapping one leg around his hips, pulling him closer. He ground his body against hers, letting her feel the hard, hot, demanding part of him, and she groaned into his mouth, feeding the frenzy.

The staff was gone for the night. The house was theirs. And in the dancing, firelit shadows, he shoved the hem of her T-shirt up so that he could cup her breasts. Through the fragile lace of her bra, he stroked his thumbs across her nipples, eliciting a moan of pleasure from Teresa's throat.

That soft sound stoked the fires inside him into a blaze that quickly engulfed him. Rico could hardly breathe for the need crouched in his chest. He flicked her bra open and cupped both of her breasts in his palms.

She held on to him, fingers grasping at his shoulders as she pushed herself into his touch. "Rico, more. I want more."

So did he. But he wanted her naked.

"Clothes," he murmured, letting her go briefly. "Off. Now."

"Oh, yes." Nodding, she pulled her T-shirt up and over her head, then tossed it aside. He watched her step out of her shorts, displaying the lacy, pale pink thong she wore beneath them.

His mouth went dry and his pulse skyrocketed. He kept his gaze locked with hers as he quickly tore off his own clothing and threw it to the floor. When he was naked, her gaze dropped to his erection and she sighed in anticipation.

She reached out one hand to curl her fingers around him and he hissed in a breath at the first touch of her hand. She smiled up into his eyes and stroked, rubbed and caressed him until his eyes were rolling back in his head and he had to fight for every breath.

Body taut, tension coiled, he was so close to exploding he couldn't risk her fingers on him another minute. He caught her hand in his and shook his head. "Enough."

"No," she said breathlessly with a shake of her head. "It's not nearly enough."

He had to smile. His Teresa was a passionate one and he loved that about her. No simpering, coy females for him. Rico appreciated that his woman wanted as hungrily as he did.

His woman.

That thought echoed in his mind until he deliberately shut it down.

He pulled her up against him, enjoying the feel of her lush, curvy body pressed to his. Again, she hooked her leg around his waist and he felt the heat of her core against his hard length. He groaned tightly and backed her up until she bumped into the arm of the leather couch. When she went to fall back onto it, he caught her, turned her in his arms and eased her down until she was bent over, her luscious, beautiful behind displayed to him.

She propped herself up on her elbows and looked back at him over her shoulder. She wiggled her hips suggestively, licked her lips, took a breath and said, "Touch me, Rico."

Her welcome, her *passion* undid him. He reached down and tugged that thong from her and rubbed her tender flesh with strong strokes. She moaned again and pushed her hips up, bracing her feet apart on the floor, giving him easy access to drive them both over the edge.

His brain splintered, thoughts dissolving under an on-slaught of pure sensation that tore through him. Rico had never lost control of himself this way. Never allowed a woman to reach past his well-built defenses to glimpse the man he was beneath the sophisticated veneer. But Teresa did it without even trying.

Rico's finely honed control simply snapped. He couldn't wait another minute. Couldn't be denied the ecstasy of being surrounded by her wet heat. He bent over her, letting her feel how badly he wanted her. She turned her face to him and their tongues met in a fast, delving exploration, then he straightened and positioned himself behind her.

Her breath came fast and hard. She threw her hair out of her face and turned her head to watch him. Her eyes gleamed and she licked her bottom lip with a long, slow swipe of her tongue.

He ran his hands up and down her back, following the line of her spine and the curve of her behind until she was groaning with need and twisting beneath his grip.

His thumbs swiped down into the heat of her and spread her inner core to his gaze. She was hot and damp and as he stroked her she moaned, "Rico, please. Touch me. Touch me."

He did, stroking her inside and out as his own body screamed for him to enter her. To claim her as his.

Heart racing, his blood thrummed in his veins and urged him on. Teresa looked back at him again, her breath coming harder, faster, and she whispered, "Hurry."

He grinned at her eagerness. His Teresa had never been shy about lovemaking. When they were first together, they had christened every room in his suite over the Cancún hotel and what they had done on his terrace one memorable morning still woke him up at night, wanting to do it all again.

"Please," she muttered, bracing herself on the leather cushions and wiggling her hips in invitation. "Now, Rico. Do it now."

"Now," he agreed and pushed himself into her depths.

She cried out his name at his entry and everything in him fisted painfully. She was so hot, so tight and felt so right. He rocked in and out of her body, hating every retreat and welcoming every surge as the blessing it was.

Again and again, he pushed them both higher and higher, the rhythm they set breathtaking. The only sounds in the room were their heavy breathing and the hiss and snap of the fire.

He leaned over her, cupped her breasts in his hands and tweaked her nipples as his body continued to plunge into hers. She groaned and rocked back into him, doing all she could to match his movements.

She humbled him, aroused him and left him shaken to the heart of him. Desire pumped like a wildfire through his body even while his mind stood apart and realized how precious she was. How special to him. How his life would be even emptier once she was gone from it.

But Rico didn't want to think now. Didn't want to recognize future or past. All that existed was the present. This moment snatched out of time where he and Te-

resa could be who they were destined to be. Two halves
of a whole.

That thought staggered him, so he pushed it aside. He
gave himself over to the sensations cresting inside him.
Rico looked down at her and saw her bite down on her
bottom lip as she fought to claim the release that was so
close to each of them.

He felt her internal muscles clench and strain around
him and knew her climax was only moments away. He
gave her everything he had and when she shrieked his
name, he buried himself as deeply as he could inside her
and then joined her on that steep slide into completion.

Nine

When he could think again, when he could *move,* Rico gently disentangled their bodies, then helped her shift position onto his lap as he took a seat on the couch. Wrapping his arms around her, he held her carefully, as if she was fragile and likely to break.

Which, he realized, was ironic, considering what the two of them had just done. But Teresa had always brought out his protective tendencies. It seemed that had not changed. Right now she was warm and trembling in his arms, still reacting to the explosive climax that had shattered them both. And though his body was sated, Rico already wanted her again.

"That was," she said on a sigh, "*incredible.*"

"Yes, it was." He let his head drop to the back of the couch. His eyes closed and a groan lodged in his throat as he realized what had just happened. What he'd done without even thinking about it. But then, that was the problem, wasn't it? He *hadn't* been thinking at all. "It was also incredibly stupid."

"What?" She looked up at him, her hair a wild tangle around her face, her mouth puffy from his kisses and her eyes still shining with satisfaction. "What do you mean? How was any of that stupid?"

He blew out a breath and met her gaze. "I lost control."

"I know," she said, giving him a slow, sexy, very tempting smile. "I liked it."

"So did I," he admitted. He lifted his head, stared into her eyes and added, "But I didn't stop for a condom."

"Oh. *Oh*." She bit her lip, took a breath and said, "All right, that was stupid. But this wasn't only your fault, Rico. I wasn't thinking either."

"Small consolation." Rico had never lost control like that. But then, only Teresa had ever touched him so deeply that his brain shut off and let his body take over.

"If it helps any, I'm healthy." She laid one hand on his chest. "I haven't been with anyone since you."

Those words rattled around in his mind and then slipped down to center around his heart. He shouldn't have cared, but he did. Shouldn't have been pleased, but he was. For five years he had imagined his *wife,* thinking herself divorced, being with other men. Letting them kiss her, taste her. Giving to them what had been only his. To know that none of those torturous imaginings had been real was a gift he hadn't expected.

He dropped one hand to the curve of her breast and slowly stroked his fingertips across one hard, dusky nipple. She sighed in reaction and he felt his groin leap to life again. So did she and she smiled knowingly. That small smile touched something inside him that he didn't want to explore too closely.

It was enough that she was here. With him. For right now. He hadn't looked to the future since the night she'd disappeared from the hotel in Mexico. Instead, his thoughts had always gone back to when she had been there beside him. Smiling, laughing, giving him a secretive look that told him she wanted him as badly as he wanted her.

Rico had never planned on giving her a confession about their time apart, but since she had been so open with him, he could do no less and still retain any sense of honor in his own mind. If he was honest with himself, he would have to say that he'd enjoyed having her think that he had moved on to other women. But now, especially with what had just happened between them and with her admission, he couldn't let her go on believing his lie of omission.

Lie. He was only now seeing that as much as he hated being lied to himself, he was as guilty as anyone when it came to convenient untruths.

"I have not been with anyone since you, either." He watched surprise flash in her eyes and pleasure quickly followed.

"But—" She shook her head. "All of the pictures of you with models and actresses…"

"Things are not always what they seem." He ran one hand up and down her bare back in long, slow strokes, loving the feel of her skin beneath his palm.

"All right, then answer me this." She took a breath, blew it out, and asked, "Why haven't you been with any of those women?"

He laughed shortly. "Because unlike you, I *knew* I was still married."

She flushed and the soft color filling her cheeks made her look even lovelier, though he wouldn't have thought that possible.

"And you?" he countered. "What kept you from other men?"

She was silent for several long, tense seconds before she said, "You're the only man I wanted."

Heat spilled through him instantly. He realized that he *wanted* to believe her. He wanted to think that she had missed him as desperately as he had missed her for the last five years. But if she felt so strongly about him, how could she disappear from his life? How could she have lied to him about who she was? And how could she have stayed away for so long?

She leaned her head against his chest and he knew she could hear his heartbeat slamming against his ribs. Since she'd arrived on Tesoro, Teresa had tried to explain her past actions to him and he hadn't been interested in listening. Now, though, he wanted to know. Needed to hear her explanation, whatever it was. And yet he had to wonder if he would be able to believe her.

His mind was a rushing torrent of contradictory thoughts. His blood burned in his veins. His body was hard and ready to take her again.

What this woman could do to him was dangerous.

What he had just done to her, he reminded himself, was unforgivable. Even if they were both healthy, he thought, no condom meant there was a chance at an unexpected pregnancy. And they had to talk about the possibilities.

"Teresa," he said softly, turning her face up to his. "I must know. Are you taking birth control?"

"No." She shook her head, then laid her hand over his, holding his hand to her breast. "I'm not. But don't worry, Rico. Everything will be fine. What are the odds I could be pregnant from one time?"

It depended on whether or not the gods had a sense of humor, he supposed. He remembered how not too long ago he'd actually imagined Teresa pregnant with his child. Now, through his own stupidity, there was a chance that would happen.

"I was never much of a gambler, because the odds are usually against you." He shook his head, still having a hard time believing that he had put them in this position. "I must apologize to you. For losing control of myself."

"Don't," she said, meeting his eyes. "Don't you dare apologize. I wanted this. I wanted you. I'm glad you lost control, Rico, and if I am pregnant…we'll deal with the situation if it presents itself."

Deal with it.

He didn't know exactly what she meant by that, but he knew very well what would happen if she was pregnant with his child. They would stay married. The divorce he'd promised her would never happen.

And that would mean he would have to find a way to live with the still-rich memories of her betrayal. His chest tightened as if iron bands were wrapped around his body, squeezing mercilessly.

How could he spend his life with a woman he couldn't trust? Would he ask himself every day if *today* was the day she would bolt?

Shaking his head, he wrapped his arms around his

wife and wondered if passion would be enough to save a marriage born in deception.

A few days later Teresa and Rico went into the village to shop for gifts for Melinda and her new son.

The day was warm, the wind was soft and two of the small launches used to transport guests from St. Thomas were docked at the harbor.

Tesoro village looked, Teresa thought, like a movie set. It was too perfect to be real. The street was narrow and lined on either side by brightly painted shops. From pastels to jewel tones, each building was as different as the wares it offered.

There was a bakery, and the scent of cinnamon wafted through its open door to tempt pedestrians. There were souvenir shops, a chocolatier that Teresa really wanted to visit, and every other kind of shop you could imagine, all catering to the wealthy tourists who came to the island to vacation. At the end of the winding street there was a small grocery store that mostly served the locals and there was a spectacular view of the ocean from every point on the tidy street. The shops huddled close to the freshly swept sidewalks. Windows gleamed, reflecting the bright light of the sun, and terra-cotta pots positioned outside the tidy stores held trailing bouquets of brightly colored flowers.

There was so much to see, Teresa swung her head from side to side in an attempt to miss nothing. "It's so pretty," she said, with a glance up at Rico, walking beside her. "Like a postcard."

"That's been said," he agreed. "In fact, Sean and I hired photographers to take photos of this street at different angles and at different times of the year. Then Walter picked the ones he liked and we had postcards made to be sold in all of the shops. Proceeds go directly to the island, and the citizens here vote on how the money's spent."

She just stared at him for a moment, letting the surprise she felt show on her features. "In Mexico you stayed out of local politics. Said you only wanted to run your hotel. You weren't interested in joining committees or getting involved with the other hoteliers or the tourist industry."

He shrugged and shifted his gaze to pass over the main street, now crowded with a few of the tourists staying at his hotel. "Everything changes."

She sighed, staring up at his profile. "Not everything," she murmured, knowing that her feelings for him would never change. Of course, she also knew that Rico wouldn't believe her even if she was foolish enough to admit to still loving him. So she kept that piece of information to herself.

"There were two boats in the harbor," she pointed out. "I mean, besides the local fishing boats."

He nodded, tucked her arm through his and started walking again. "Sometimes there are more hotel guests coming in from St. Thomas than usual."

"No cruise ships are allowed to stop here, right?"

He glanced at her. "How did you know that?"

Well, because when she found out that Rico had bought land on Tesoro with the intention of building a hotel, she'd spent a lot of time researching the island. She'd wanted at least to know what he was doing and where he would be living—even if she couldn't be with him. Which was how she had known that Melinda's grandfather owned the island outright. And that it was one of the bigger privately held islands in the Caribbean.

Walter liked keeping his island as private as possible, but he also was aware that the shopkeepers needed to make a living. So he'd compromised and allowed small ships to bring in tourists to stay in the hotel and give the islanders a steady income while at the same time protecting Tesoro from being overrun with too many people.

When she first read about him and his stubborn refusal to welcome cruise ships, she had thought the older man was shortsighted, not letting his island progress. But looking at the village now, she could appreciate his decision. She imagined these tidy streets jam-packed with crowds of people—snapping pictures, drinking too much, dropping trash on the pretty streets—and actually shuddered at the mental image. Walter had been smart to protect this place.

Now, to answer Rico's question, she hedged a little. "I read up on the island when I found out my father and brother had come here."

He scowled at her and she was sorry to see that bringing up her family had instantly soured his mood. But better that than letting him know she'd been keeping tabs on him for years.

"I admit, I was surprised that your family chose to come here for a 'job.'" Rico started walking again and Teresa kept pace. "It's a small island—thieves are spotted more easily, and, as it turns out, *caught* more easily, as well."

True, her father's ego would be bruised for years over Rico actually catching him. Police departments all around the world had been trying and failing to do it for years.

But Rico was different. As tenacious as he was, she had known that coming into contact with him again would bring disaster down on the Corettis. Which was exactly why she had warned her family off. Rico King was nobody's fool. His eyes were too sharp to miss anything and he wasn't one of those wealthy types who only occasionally stepped in to keep an eye on what belonged to him. Rico was hands-on. He would know everything happening with his properties.

Especially since he'd been robbed himself, he was on a higher alert than most people would have been.

Still, she hadn't been all that surprised when her father and brother had come to Tesoro.

"My father enjoys a challenge," she said, and couldn't help the small smile that curved her mouth. Whatever else Dominick Coretti was, he had always been a warm and loving father.

"He should try *not* stealing then," Rico told her flatly. "Give himself a real challenge."

"Don't think I haven't suggested it." Teresa lifted her face into the wind and sighed as the cool air slid past. "But…"

"Once a thief, always a thief?"

Teresa let that statement go because it was pointless to argue with him about the Coretti family business. He would never understand the centuries-old legacy that Dominick was so determined to keep alive. Teresa's worry was that her father wasn't getting any younger and perhaps his skills weren't as good as they had been once—though she would never suggest such a thing to him in person.

She didn't want to see her family in prison, though. And heaven knew the Corettis had more than enough money to retire. It wasn't, she thought, the actual stealing that her father loved so much as the adventure of having every day be a different one. Of finding a way into a heavily guarded estate. Of out-thinking security parameters and disabling electronic surveillance equipment. He *liked* pitting himself against an adversary, so thinking of a way to get her father to hang up his black gloves was going to be difficult.

That was a problem for the future, though. She only had a little more than two weeks left with Rico. She could spend that time arguing with him over the Coretti family business…or she could simply enjoy what she had while she had it.

"Oh, my." She stopped dead in front of a shop window, drawing Rico to a stop, as well. "How beautiful."

In the jewelry shop window, on a bed of black velvet, sat rings, bracelets, earrings and necklaces, all set with blue-green stones that Teresa had never seen before. They shone in the sunlight like pieces of the sea, trapped forever in settings of gold and silver. Pure avarice struck her and the Coretti legacy reared its ugly head as she curled her fingers into her palms to keep from trying to grab them all right through the glass. "They're beautiful."

"They are." Rico stood beside her, but in the reflection of the glass, she saw that he was looking at her, not the jewelry. "They're Tesoro topazes. The gemstone is found only on this island."

"So jewel prospecting is a pretty good job on this island, then?"

He laughed shortly and she suddenly found his eyes even more appealing than the glittering stones and precious metals spread out in front of her. "Occasionally a hotel guest will stumble on a find while out for a hike. But the islanders know where to look for the best stones."

"It would be fun," she mused as her gaze swung back to the shop window. "Like a treasure hunt."

"The jewelry you see here is Melinda's work," he said after Teresa spent another minute or two practically drooling on the glass.

"Melinda?" Teresa looked at him.

"She makes the jewelry and it's sold here."

"She's incredibly talented," Teresa murmured. "And I think I'm more than a little envious."

"On the other hand," Rico told her, capturing her hand in his again, "you are a chef and Melinda is a miserable cook. So for survival's sake, I would choose your gifts over hers."

A flush of pride and pleasure filled her and just for a second or two she allowed herself to fully enjoy the look in his eyes and the warmth of his hand in hers. But even as she watched, the gleam in his eyes faded slightly. So she spoke up and kept her tone light.

"Well, then," Teresa said with a half smile. "Guess it would be pointless to buy her that lovely bracelet as a new-mom present. I mean, since she made it."

"True." He pulled her hand through the crook of his arm and steered her along the street after she gave one last look at the shop window. "When Sean and Melinda became engaged, he bought her a ring and only later found out that she had made it herself."

Teresa laughed at the image and enjoyed the fact that just for now, they were smiling together. Taking a walk, enjoying the day, as if reality had taken the day off. It was almost as it had been five years ago. But, of course, it couldn't last.

When Rico's cell phone rang, she felt a quick flash

of annoyance. Just when things were going so well. She stopped and waited as he glanced at the screen.

"It is the hotel," he said, then answered it. "Yes?"

His gaze shot to hers and Teresa was disappointed to see his easy expression drain away to be replaced with the cold, cautious one she'd become so accustomed to.

"What is it?" Her voice was as resigned as she felt.

"A phone call," he said. "From your father. The hotel is forwarding it to my cell."

"My father?" She hadn't heard from her father since the day he left. Mainly because Rico had commandeered her cell phone—no doubt so she couldn't make escape plans. She took the phone from him and tried not to worry at what might have happened to make her father call. "Papa?"

"Bellissima, are you all right?" Nick's voice was hurried, anxious. "I have not heard from you and when I try to call your cell, I get only your answering machine."

"I, um, lost my phone," she said, with a quick look at Rico, who only seemed amused. Yes, she'd lied *again.* But she couldn't very well tell her father that Rico had commandeered her phone to ensure that she didn't call her family to plot an escape.

"Good, good. I am glad you are all right. This King person, he is treating you well?"

"I'm fine, Papa. Rico has been very..." She paused and caught his eyes. One black eyebrow lifted, as if he was waiting to see exactly what she would tell her father about their time together. "...*kind.*"

He snorted.

Her father only muttered something in Italian that she thought it was better Rico hadn't heard. Then he spoke again.

"When this is all over, *cara,* you will tell me all about how you could marry this man without telling your papa."

"I will," she promised, though she knew that conversation wouldn't be a pleasant one. No man wanted to hear that his daughter had been so swept away by passion that marrying a man she hardly knew had seemed like the rational thing to do.

"But for now," her father continued, "there is a small *problema, mi cara.*"

"Problem?" she repeated for Rico's benefit, and his scowl deepened accordingly. "What's wrong?"

Her father huffed out a breath. "We cannot find Gianni," he admitted finally. "He, too, is not answering his phone—why do my children plague me with machines they do not bother to use?—and he has not been in touch with us. He is not here in Italy and no one has seen him in weeks."

Her brother could be anywhere in the world. If he didn't want to be found, no one would be able to locate him. But why wasn't he answering his phone? It wasn't like him to simply disappear without telling the family when he would be back.

There were only two weeks left in Rico's ultimatum, and if Gianni didn't return Rico's dagger at the end of the month…the Coretti family would end up in jail. As to what Rico would do with *her,* she couldn't even guess.

"Did you try reaching him at his apartment in London?" she asked, keeping her gaze now firmly away from Rico's.

"*Si, si.* Of course we tried. Paulo is traveling, trying to run Gianni to ground." He sounded completely disgusted with the whole situation. "Paulo is in Monaco right now. If he finds Gianni there, he will call me immediately. I am going to Gstaad. He had a woman there last year and perhaps…"

That was the trouble with having a wandering family. They all had connections all over the world. Gianni could be anywhere. But the fact that he wasn't answering his phone had Teresa more than a little worried. What if he had been arrested somewhere? What if he was right now sitting in a jail cell and *couldn't* call?

She chewed at her bottom lip as she considered the possibilities. Then she realized that if one of the Coretti family had been arrested, it would have made all of the news programs. So clearly Gianni wasn't in jail. So where, exactly, was he?

"Papa, if you can't find him in Switzerland," she said, "call Simone in Paris. She might know where he is."

"Ah, of course!" Her father sounded joyful at the suggestion. "Simone and Gianni…" And off he went again in fluent, musical Italian.

Teresa stole a glance at Rico and was sorry she had. He didn't look happy. His blue eyes were almost cobalt and a muscle in his tightly clenched jaw twitched with his effort to control his anger.

"You will be well, *bellissima,*" her father said when he had wound down. "All will be taken care of. But we *might* need a little more time…"

Oh, no. "Hold on, Papa."

Taking a breath, she covered the phone with her hand and spoke to the man glowering beside her. "Paulo and my father are having a hard time finding Gianni," she explained.

"He's the one who took my dagger?"

"Yes," she said shortly. "And it seems he's disappeared, at least *temporarily.* They're looking for him, but Papa says they might need a little more time and—"

Shaking his head, he snatched his phone from her and said tightly, "Signore Coretti. You have no more time. There are two weeks left. If my dagger is not returned, the evidence I hold goes to Interpol."

She could hear her father's loud blustering and his shouted demand, "And what of Teresa? What happens to my little girl?"

She held her breath, waiting for the answer to that question. Rico's gaze met hers and she saw no softening in those cold blue depths. No warmth on his features when he said, "She will no longer be your concern. As she is my *wife,* I decide what will happen."

He shut off the phone and dropped it into his shirt pocket. Looking down at her, he repeated, "Two weeks, Teresa."

"And then?"

"We will see when the time comes." He took her hand in his, but it wasn't a comforting grip. More like a jailer's hold on a flight risk. "For now, let us go to the chocolatier for Melinda's gift."

She followed after him because she had no choice. But the truth was, she'd have followed him anyway.

There were only two weeks left. And whatever his plan for Teresa entailed, she knew it didn't include staying with him.

So while her family panicked and searched the globe for Gianni…Teresa was going to try to enjoy the moments she had left with the only man she'd ever love.

Ten

Two days later, Rico arrived home earlier than usual.

Ever since that phone call from Dominick, there'd been new tension between him and Teresa. It was as if they both realized that time was running out and neither of them knew quite how it would end.

Over the last couple of weeks so much had changed between them that Rico wasn't comfortable with his old plan of revenge and payback. Now he was more focused on Teresa herself and what they might have found together. Though the complication of the Corettis still stood between them.

He knew she was worried about her family. Anxious at the thought of her brothers and father going to prison. And yes, he knew that it was his threats that had brought them all to this point.

The difference was that now he hated to see her on

edge. Hated knowing that it was because of *him* that she had to fear for her family. And he really hated that he was falling under her spell again.

He couldn't trust her, but that didn't seem to matter. Old feelings were back and they were growing into something even bigger than they'd once been.

Scrubbing one hand across his face and then shoving that hand through his hair, he tried to find a way through this mess of his own design. But there was nothing. He had backed himself into a corner.

Moving quietly through his darkened house, he headed unerringly for the bedroom where Teresa would be waiting for him. A sharp tug of pleasure dragged at the edges of his heart at the knowledge. Oh, he was in deep trouble.

His steps faltered as he heard low-pitched voices—one of them a man's—coming from his bedroom. Rico went instantly still. Someone was in his bedroom, with Teresa. What the hell? She wasn't screaming for help, which only fed the flames of suspicion burning inside. On alert now, he eased closer to the partially closed door and peered inside.

Everything in him urged Rico to charge into that room and find out who the mystery bastard was. But this time his mind won over his instincts. He had to know what was going on and if he slammed in, the hurried conversation would end. So instead he moved closer and listened.

"Bastien, you have to *go*," Teresa said, her voice hurried, yet determined.

"Not without you." The man's voice was deep and adamant.

Rico's blood rushed to his head and he curled his fists at his sides. But before he could give in to the jealousy pouring through him as though from a tap turned on full blast, Rico peered into the room and saw an older man, dressed all in black. His gray mustache covered half his face and his bushy gray brows were wiry.

So, not a romantic encounter.

"Your father sent me to get you away," the man insisted, tossing a nervous glance over his shoulder at the open terrace doors. "He cannot find Gianni or the dagger."

Teresa sighed. "My brother wasn't in Paris, either?"

"No." The old man lowered his voice even further, but his insistence was sharp. "We are still looking, but your father does not wish you to stay with this man— your husband—any longer. He worries for your safety."

Rico scowled at the door. As if he was a danger to Teresa? Insult slammed into him but was buried deep as he waited for her reply.

"Tell my father I'm safe, Bastien. And I can't leave the island."

"*Si,* you can. I have a fishing boat waiting at the harbor." The older man reached out and took her hand. "From the mainland, we board the plane your father has waiting. It will take us to him."

Anger flared so bright and hot, Rico could hardly see. Teeth clenched, his jaw muscles felt tight enough to snap. He could already feel what would happen next. Teresa was going to do it again. She would run to save her family. She would break her word and disappear. Again.

He took a step forward, intending to stop her before she got one step outside his house, but he halted suddenly when Teresa spoke.

"You don't understand, Bastien," she said, words tumbling from her in a rush. "I *won't* leave. I gave my word to Rico and I won't break it. Not again. He's my husband

and I...*care* for him. I won't hurt him by disappearing one more time, Bastien. I agreed to stay here for a month and I'm going to."

Rico laid one hand on the doorjamb to steady himself. His world had just been rocked. Teresa had shocked him straight to the bone. She cared for him. *Love?* Did she still love him? While he stood there outside the room, something flickered to life in the center of his chest. Warmth filled him along with the territorial urge to go to her, hold her tightly to him and sweep her into bed, where he would damn well *keep* her for the rest of their time together.

He shifted position slightly so he could see Teresa better. Her long, thick hair was pulled back into a ponytail at the back of her neck. She was wearing the dark green nightgown he loved to strip from her, with a short white robe over it, loosely belted at her waist. Her long, tanned legs were bare and planted wide apart as if in a fighting stance. But it was the expression on her face that caught and held his attention. She looked...fierce. She was defying her father's attempt at a rescue. In favor of Rico.

This time she had chosen *him.*

"Your father will not be happy." The older man was speaking again.

"My father is the one who taught me that once your word is given, it is sacred," Teresa told him. "I won't cheat Rico. Tell my father to find Gianni. He still has two weeks to bring the dagger here."

Through the anger at Dominick's duplicity rose a new and unexpected feeling inside Rico. Trust. That warmth rushing through him was enveloping as he watched the woman who was his wife. And though he warned himself to be wary, he knew that something between them had shifted tonight.

Gathering together the threads of his anger, Rico pushed the door open and stepped into the room. Both Teresa and the older man whipped around to face him. She looked stunned and embarrassed. The man she'd called Bastien just looked worried. As he should.

"Get out," Rico said, voice tight with the effort of holding on to the anger churning in his gut.

The man didn't need to be told twice. He scuttled for the terrace doors and only stopped at the threshold when Rico spoke up again.

"Leave the island tonight," he advised. "If I see you here tomorrow I'll have you arrested for trespassing."

One bob of the man's head told Rico he was understood. In another second, the man was gone and he and Teresa were alone in the room.

"I can explain," she said quickly.

"You don't have to." Rico looked down at her and felt that rush of warmth again. She was beautiful. She was proud and defiant and she was his. For now, anyway. "I heard everything before I came in. Your father sent him."

She blew out a breath before lifting her chin high enough that she met his gaze. "Yes. Bastien is a family friend. Sort of an honorary uncle, I guess."

"Uh-huh." Despite everything, he felt a quick flash of irritation for Nick Coretti. Yet how could he blame the man for trying to save his daughter? Rico or any of the Kings would have done the same for one of their family. Though it burned that the older man had almost put one over on him. Would have, if Teresa hadn't chosen to stay.

"So your father arranged this *escape*."

"He's worried about me," Teresa told him with a heavy

sigh of frustration mingled with exasperation. "He can't find Gianni or the dagger."

"Are you certain that it is *you* he's worried about?" he asked. "Or is he more concerned with the idea that he and his sons are going to prison?"

She flushed and a spark of anger lit her eyes briefly. "Of course he's thinking about that, too. But sending Bastien was about *me*."

Scowling, Rico said, "Maybe. But it was a foolish thing to do."

He pulled his phone from his pocket, handed it to her and said, "Call him."

She took a deep breath and held it. Then she punched in her father's number and listened to it ring. "Papa?" She flicked a glance at Rico. "Yes, Bastien was here. I wouldn't go with him."

Rico heard the older man's shout and almost smiled. He, too, hated it when a plan fell apart. As his own plan concerning Teresa had, he thought grimly. But he'd consider that and the ramifications later. For now...

"Let me talk to him." He held out one hand and waited until Teresa slapped the phone onto his palm. Dominick was still shouting at his daughter when Rico interrupted him.

"Do not try something like that again," he warned, holding Teresa's gaze while he listened to Nick Coretti sputter.

"She is my daughter. I want her safe," Nick said finally.

"I understand that," Rico told him, and he meant it. He would do whatever he had to do to keep a member of *his* family safe. But that didn't mean he was going to let Nick off the hook. "Teresa is safe with me. But if you try to get her off the island again, I'll make sure you and your sons are locked up forever."

The man on the other end of the line was quiet for a long moment, then said, "Agreed."

"Good." Rico looked into Teresa's eyes and added for both her and her father's benefit, "I am a man of my word. At the end of the month, once I have my dagger, I'll hand over the evidence I hold."

"And," Nick said firmly, "you will release my daughter."

He should. It was part of the deal he'd made. Not to mention the fact that he had spent the last five years working to get his errant wife out of his mind and heart. But now, looking at Teresa, Rico knew that he couldn't let her go.

Yes, he'd given his word. But he couldn't, *wouldn't* let Teresa leave him and disappear again. She was a part of him. A part of his life here on the island and without her...no.

It was unthinkable. But he couldn't very well say that to her father. So instead he said only, "We made a deal. I will stick to it—as you should."

He ended the call and felt the world beneath his feet tilt precariously. All his life Rico had done his best to be a man of his word. To avoid lies and deception. And now the only way he could get out of a bargain he had struck was to break every one of his personal rules.

Which meant he had to find another way out of this.

"He's scared," Teresa said as explanation, dragging him out of his thoughts and back to the present.

"I know." He reached for her before he could stop himself, cupping her cheek in the palm of his hand. "Any father would be. What I want to hear is why you didn't go with Bastien."

She was silent for a few seconds, as if she was considering just how to say what she needed to say. Finally she said quietly, "Five years ago, I made the choice I thought I had to. But tonight I didn't want to repeat the same mistake."

He stiffened slightly, as he always did when reminded of that time five years past. He'd shut her down whenever she had tried to tell him about the night she had left. He hadn't wanted to hear this before, but now he needed to. Rico had to know why she'd left him. Why she'd run— so he could believe that she wouldn't do the same now.

The bedroom was cool and dimly lit from the moonlight pouring in through the open terrace doors and the twin bedside lamps casting golden light across the bed and floor.

"Tell me." His words were short and clipped, but they seemed to release her from a tension that had coiled inside her for too long.

When her eyes met his again, they were damp, looking like gold coins drenched in water. If her tears spilled over, it would tear at his heart, he knew. Rico steadied himself, then took her hand and led her to the bed. Sitting down, he drew her with him and repeated, "Tell me."

"I'm glad you're finally willing to listen."

"I wasn't ready before," he told her. "I am now."

Nodding, Teresa tried to smile, but gave that up quickly. "All right, but first you have to know that when I was eighteen, I told my father that I wasn't going to be a thief. That I wanted a different kind of life."

He hadn't expected to hear that and as he thought about it, he laughed shortly.

She glared at him.

"Sorry," he muttered. "I was just imagining how your father must have taken that decision."

A reluctant smile curved her mouth. "Not well. He was horrified. And disappointed. But in the end, though he didn't understand my decision, he respected it."

Rico silently gave Nick Coretti half a point of admiration for backing off and giving his daughter the room she needed to grow her own way. Not that he was willing to forgive the old thief or anything.

"I took that job at your hotel," she said, starting off slowly, her soft voice hesitant, as if she wasn't sure how to put it now that he'd given her the chance. "And I asked my family to stay away." She smiled wryly. "Usually they did as I asked, not wanting to bring down suspicion on me in a place where I happened to be working. But that was before I took a job with Rico King."

She shook her head and caught his eyes again. "The temptation was too much. The richness of your guests at the Castello de King was enough of a draw all on its own, but there was more. They knew about your dagger. There had been some piece written about it—"

Rico remembered that. Someone had done an interview with him for a national magazine article on the Cancún Castello and during the meeting the reporter had seen the Aztec dagger in a case on his desk. There had been questions and photos and apparently that had been enough to attract the attention of professional thieves.

He hadn't worried about it at the time, because his security at the hotel was top-of-the-line. But the Corettis, he was discovering, were very worthy adversaries. "I remember that article. Go on."

She nodded and threaded her fingers together in her

lap, restlessly tugging at them until he laid one hand on top of hers to hold her still.

"My oldest brother, Gianni, loves antiquities. He couldn't resist the lure of that dagger and where he went, so did my father and Paulo." She looked up at him again and held on to his hand tightly. "I swear I didn't know they were going to hit the hotel until after it was done."

Staring into those wide-open, pale brown eyes shining with misery and regret, he could only nod. Rico believed her. But then, if he hadn't been in such pain over losing her, he would have believed her long ago.

Satisfied, she kept talking. "When you discovered the dagger missing, I just…had a feeling. Then you contacted the police and were vowing to hunt down the thieves no matter what it took."

He remembered that, too. His fury at being robbed. The crushing need to retrieve something his father had passed on to him.

"While you were with the police, I searched through the guest register and found my family under one of their more familiar assumed names."

Familiar. Assumed. She had grown up quite differently than he had. Now he saw that lying, to Teresa, had been second nature. Just the way things were done. And he had to admire her for breaking away from the only life she had ever known. What kind of strength was that, to turn your back on your family? Your legacy?

"Gianni was already gone with the dagger," she was saying and Rico came out of his thoughts to listen to the rest of the story.

"My father and Paulo were packing." She winced. "They had already sent what they'd taken from your guests by overnight mail to our home in London."

And those, Rico told himself, were diamonds, rubies and emeralds that would never see the light of day again. *At least,* he told himself wryly, *not in their original settings.*

"I begged my father to call Gianni, to get him to return the dagger, but it was too late. My brother had boarded a plane right after—" She broke off.

"Right after stealing from me," Rico finished for her.

"Yes. There was no way to reach him and I'm not sure I would have been able to convince him to return the dagger even if I could have talked to him." She sighed and shook her head, pulling one hand from his to push a stray lock of hair behind her ear. "Maybe if I had confessed that we were married—" she mused. "But I just couldn't do it. You were furious, I knew I would have to leave you and there wasn't a point in telling my family and hurting my father over a marriage that would be ending anyway."

He gritted his teeth and she saw him fight for control. When he finally found it, he spoke again. "This explains the robbery," Rico said quietly. "And why you didn't tell your family about us. It does not tell me why you ran from me. Why you chose them over what we had together."

She pulled in one long, shuddering breath and slid off the bed to stand up. Facing him, she wrapped her arms around her middle, accidentally opening the fall of her robe, giving Rico a glimpse of luscious, tanned skin and the tops of her breasts beneath her nightgown. He had to force himself to focus on what she was saying.

"I left my father and Paulo packing and went back to our suite. Do you remember how you were? What you were saying?"

"No," he said. All he recalled clearly was the helpless

anger that had had him in a choke hold, strangling him with a sense of helplessness that no King could accept.

"I do," she said softly. "You told me that if it was the last thing you ever did, you would hunt down those thieves. You would see them in prison for a lifetime." She tightened her grip around her middle and held on as if clutching a lifeline in a choppy sea. "You said you would do whatever it took. That you and I would find them. Together. Then you asked if I had seen anything, heard anything unusual around the hotel."

"And you lied to me."

"Yes." She swallowed hard and nodded. "I lied. To protect my family."

"Why, Teresa?" he asked, though he already knew the answer. Her father. Her brothers. Her connection with them ran deep. Perhaps deeper than the link she had had with a new husband and the promise of a future too vague to be real.

"Because I couldn't help you track them down, Rico. I couldn't do what you needed me to do, but I couldn't stay and *not* help you, either. I would have been living a lie every day, praying that you wouldn't discover my secret." She shook her head so wildly her ponytail swung behind her head like a pendulum. "It was a disaster. Any choice I made, I hurt someone I loved. I didn't want to lie to you, but I thought that *one* lie was better than a lifetime of them."

"You should have told me," he said, pushing up from the bed to lay both hands on her shoulders. "You should have trusted me."

She laughed now and the sound wasn't musical at all. It was like shards of glass being ground under steel wheels.

"Trusted you? I should have told you that the thieves were my family and please don't prosecute?"

He frowned at her as her words resonated inside him.

"Would you have believed that I had nothing to do with the theft?" she demanded, all traces of tears gone from her eyes now, replaced by sparks of rising temper. "The first thing you said to me when you found me here was that you thought I had married you only to give my family access to your blasted dagger."

Now it was his turn to feel a rush of shame. Yes, he had convinced himself years ago that Teresa had only married him to help her family's thieving. But that had never made sense and he'd known it even while he'd allowed the thought to drive him insane. The Corettis were, if nothing else, *excellent* thieves. They didn't need to use Teresa. They'd gotten past his security and out of the country almost before he'd known he'd been hit.

No, blaming Teresa had been his pride talking. The wound she'd left when she disappeared had festered until that convenient lie he'd told himself had simply been a way of deflecting the truth.

That she'd chosen another over him.

"You're right," he said, his voice hardly more than a hush.

She blinked at him and shook her head. "Excuse me?"

One corner of his mouth lifted briefly. Of course she would be surprised. He hadn't given her any reason to think he would be on her side in *any* argument.

"I said, you are right. I would have accused you. I would have been wrong, though." He slid his hands up to hold her face between his palms. His gaze bored into hers as he willed her to believe him. "I know you weren't a part of it. And I can even understand a little now why you made the choice you did."

She huffed out a breath. "Thank you."

"But I need to know why you chose differently tonight, Teresa."

Leaning into him, she said solemnly, "Because I didn't want to hurt you again, Rico. Because this time *you* were more important. This time I had to trust you."

"Good answer," he murmured and bent down to kiss her. He'd meant only to plant a brief, hard kiss on her lips.

But at the moment of contact, Teresa wrapped her arms around him and held on. She opened her mouth and tangled her tongue with his and they were linked, as they were meant to be, always.

Rico groaned and held her tighter. Lifting her off her feet, he turned back to the bed, laid her down and then lay down beside her. Rising up on one elbow, he looked down into golden-brown eyes. Then he kissed her again and lost himself in the arms of the only woman in the world who held his heart.

Rico met Sean for lunch at a small restaurant near the harbor. It had been two days since Teresa had turned down a chance at escape. Two days since she had chosen *him* over her family. He liked knowing that she was on his side in this, but he had to wonder how long that would last if her family didn't return the dagger.

Because if that happened, he would go through with his threat. He would hand over all of the evidence he'd collected over the last several years to Interpol. And once he did that, he would lose Teresa. How could he expect her to stay with the man who had imprisoned her family? No, he knew damn well she would never forgive him for that.

And if they *did* deliver the dagger as promised, then he would have to hold up his end of the bargain and not only release Teresa, but divorce her, as well. He couldn't keep her here without going back on his word and couldn't let her go without losing a piece of his soul.

Time was ticking past. With every beat of his heart, that internal clock moved on, pushing them toward the end of the month. Toward the end of his time with Teresa.

He couldn't stand that thought.

This month had started out with him holding her against her will, yes. But that had changed, hadn't it? She didn't act like a hostage—with the run of the island, working in the hotel kitchen, coming to his bed eagerly. Whatever it was that was still humming between them, it was something that would die the moment he sent her family to prison.

"You look like hell." Sean sat back in his chair and sipped at a bottle of beer.

"Thank you. It is good to have family to turn to in times of trouble." Rico picked up his own beer and took a long swallow, hoping to ease the knot in his throat. It didn't work. "How are Melinda and Stryker?"

Sean's grin lit up his face. "Great. Seriously great." He shook his head. "The baby's keeping us both up all night, every night, but I don't even mind. Right now I'm like a zombie, but I've never had so much fun."

A pang of envy rippled through Rico, but he ignored it. No point in wishing for things that weren't going to happen. *Unless,* a voice in his mind whispered, *Teresa is already pregnant. Then your problems are over, aren't they? You stay married. You keep her with you. And you have the family you've always craved.*

He straightened in his chair as that nebulous idea took root in his mind.

"So." Sean spoke up and Rico came out of his thoughts. "You said you wanted to talk. What's going on?"

"That is a question with too many answers."

"Pick one."

"I am trying to decide what to do about Teresa."

"Ah," Sean said, smothering a laugh. "The brilliant plan falling apart? Wow. Wish I'd seen that coming. Oh. Wait. I *did*."

Rico sneered at his cousin. "Very helpful, thank you. There is nothing better than an *I told you so* at just the right moment."

"Happy to help." Sean reached for a nacho loaded with beans and cheese, then popped it into his mouth, crunching with a grin on his face.

"Right." He should have known his cousin would love this. A King liked nothing better than an entertaining "I was right, you were wrong" chat. Shaking his head, he leaned forward, bracing his arms on the glass-topped table. The bright yellow table umbrella shaded them from the noonday sun and all around them hotel guests were either boarding day boats for fishing trips or sitting at the bar having tropical drinks. "Her father hired a man to help her escape. Seems he hasn't found her brother yet and he wants more time."

"Escape? Okay, I'm guessing she didn't go anywhere, yes?"

"She stayed." Rico took a sip of his beer. "She wouldn't leave."

"Interesting." Sean smiled, then narrowed his eyes.

"Aside from the failed rescue, do you think her father's stalling deliberately?"

"It's possible," Rico admitted, thinking back to the sound of Dominick Coretti's outraged voice. "But I don't know that he would take this kind of risk with his family. So if I assume he really does need the extra time, what do I do about it?"

"What do you want to do?"

Rico sent his cousin an exasperated glare. "If I knew that, would I be asking for your opinion?"

Sean laughed. "Okay, no. I'm no fan of Teresa's family—they're thieves." He shrugged. "But you locking up her family isn't going to score you points with her, either."

"Yes, I know that, as well." Talking to his cousin was supposed to help him straighten out his thoughts.

"So go with your gut, Rico." Sean was still smiling. "You want Teresa. She wants her family safe. Do what you have to do to make everyone happy."

"Let the thieves go free?"

"It's family, man," Sean said, smile fading into a thoughtful frown. "Look at the Kings. What haven't we been willing to do to keep family safe?"

He was right, Rico knew. And the answer, it seemed, was simple after all. A King would risk anything for family. And Teresa—not to mention the child she might be carrying—was his family.

Eleven

Another week of her month was gone and Teresa felt as though she was listening to the inexorable tick of a countdown in her head. Every morning she woke up beside Rico and every evening the heat between them sizzled anew. And every day gone was one less that she had with him.

Sitting on a chaise on the beach below Rico's house, Teresa curled her feet up under her on the floral cushion. She swept her gaze across Rico's private slice of the Tesoro paradise and sighed. A yacht was docked at Rico's private pier and the brass fittings winked in the bright sunlight. "Oh, God, I don't want to leave."

She loved it here. Loved the easy, relaxed way of life on the island. She loved having the wild beauty surrounding her wherever she went. She loved working in the hotel and she'd already made some good friends here. The hotel staff, Sean and Melinda.

But mostly she loved being with Rico. For so long she'd yearned to be with him again and now it was as if she was living in a perfect dream world.

But the sad part about dreams was that eventually you woke up and the dream shattered.

A wind off the ocean buffeted her, waves crashed against the shore, sending spray into the air, and Rico's boat creaked noisily as it rose and fell with the surging sea. Out on the horizon, dark clouds gathered, promising a coming storm, and birds in the tree behind her chattered as if in warning.

The wind kicked up, sending grains of sand stinging into her skin like tiny bullets. She hardly noticed since the pain around her heart went so much deeper.

What was she going to do without Rico in her life?

"I was looking for you."

His deep voice coming from right behind her didn't surprise Teresa. It was as if she'd conjured Rico out of thin air just by thinking about him. She hoped it would work that well in the coming years, but somehow she doubted it.

"You weren't worried, were you?" She tipped her head back and shaded her eyes with one hand. "I thought I already proved to you that I'm not going to leave the island before the end of the month."

He sank into a crouch beside her and reached out one hand to tuck her hair behind her ear. That one slight touch sent shivers of anticipation rattling through her body. He gave her a half smile and shook his head.

"You did," he said with a nod. "You gave me your word. I wasn't worried. I just wanted to see if you'd like to take a ride around the island."

His hair blew in the ever-present wind, the white shirt

he wore was open at the throat and the sleeves were rolled up. His black jeans looked worn and comfortable. He was also barefoot and, for some reason, that only heightened his sex appeal. The man was a walking orgasm.

"With you?"

He gave her another half smile. "No. With Sean."

"Funny." She nodded, held out one hand to him and let him help her up from the chair.

For the last week, Rico had been attentive, seductive and *romantic* in a way she hadn't experienced since they were first together. Every day he had a new adventure for the two of them. They had spent one day out on his yacht, alternately swimming in the ocean and climbing aboard to dry off and make love. They'd had a romantic seaside dinner in the village and finished the evening off by dancing in the moonlight. One day he had even taken her treasure hunting for Tesoro topazes.

There had been picnics on the beach and lazy swings in the hammock. Long walks and sitting together at night in front of a fire built more for romance than warmth.

It had been a perfect week. Perfect in ways that made her miserable to think of losing Rico forever. But in all the time they had spent together, not once had he talked about the possibility of her staying. Not once had he hinted he *wanted* her to stay. And not once had he said that he didn't want the divorce he had promised her.

So though she was being romanced, she had finally figured out that Rico was simply saying goodbye to her. A long, drawn-out, incredibly sweet and romantic goodbye.

And that broke her heart.

Still, she wouldn't let him see that she knew what he was doing. Wouldn't let him know that her heart ached to be with him. That the thought of leaving made her feel as though she had been hollowed out and left an empty shell.

If he could make these last few days together special, then the least she could do was join him in the pretense. There would be plenty of time later for the tears that seemed to be constantly near the surface. So for now she smiled up at him and let him see only the pleasure she felt at being beside him. "Are we going in a car or on your boat?"

"For what I want to show you, we'll have to take the car."

"I'd love to."

She bent to pick up her sandals and then followed him from the beach and across the manicured lawn to the driveway in front of his home. A small red sports car sat in the shade of several trees, waiting for them.

Once they were in the car and buckled in, Rico fired up the engine and steered the car out of the driveway and down to the main road. But instead of heading toward the hotel and the village, he turned left and sped along the narrow, paved road.

"You've been here nearly three weeks," he said, his voice carrying over the growl of the engine. "And I thought you might like to see the rest of the island."

Before you go.

He didn't say it, but he didn't have to. She knew exactly what he meant. A bubble of pain opened up in the center of her chest, but Teresa fought it down. Being here with Rico was too nice to spoil with thoughts of what was going to happen all too soon.

"Thanks. I would."

She'd seen a lot of Tesoro from his boat and he had taken her to the foot of the hills to search for topaz. But there was still so much she hadn't seen. Still so much she hadn't done. Leaving tore at her and she turned away from him so he wouldn't see the sorrow in her eyes.

Instead, she looked at the landscape as they passed. As they got farther from the village and the hotel and Rico's house, the land changed, shifted. Stands of jungle were so thick the trees looked like a solid green wall. Even the sunlight barely made it through the leafy foliage. It was like driving through a green tunnel. Then they emerged into the light again and Teresa gasped at the beauty spreading out on either side of the car. Meadows with wildflowers dancing in the breeze. Patches of farmland, even a small vineyard. And at the edge of the island, a beach with sand so white it hurt the eyes to look at it and the ocean beyond.

"It's so gorgeous here." She leaned in to Rico to make sure he heard her.

He grinned, whipping his hair back from his face as he turned to smile at her. "It is. And what I'm going to show you now will take your breath away."

That happened just looking at him, Teresa thought. But she was so glad to see pleasure in his eyes, in the easy curve of his mouth, she only said, "I'm ready."

He laughed and stepped on the gas, sending the little red car hurtling along the road at a speed that brought a laugh from her throat.

The road wound on and Teresa hoped the ride would never end. She could spend eternity like this, she told herself. Beside Rico, off on an adventure together, with the wind in their hair and the sun on their faces. But eventually Rico pulled the car over and turned the engine off.

She looked around and saw a wall of rock spilling

down into a patch of trees that looked cool and shad-owed. "Where are we?"

"You'll see." He got out of the car, came around to her side and opened the door. "Just leave your sandals here. You won't need them."

Then, taking her hand, he led her into the cool shade of the stand of trees. Birds sang, the wind blew and under it all, she heard the steady roar of the ocean. But as Rico led her on, her bare feet making no sound on the sandy ground, that roar became louder and she noticed it didn't have the sighing rhythm that she'd become used to. "What is that?"

He looked at her and grinned. "One moment and you'll see for yourself."

Using a series of timeworn rocks as steps, he led her down a narrow path through the trees. The roaring sound was even louder now and Teresa thought she knew what to expect. She was only half-right.

Stepping out into a clearing, she saw the waterfall she'd guessed was their destination. But she hadn't been prepared for the sheer beauty of the place. It was de-serted. Private. Water spilled from a rock overhang into a pond below that then drained down into a river whose twists and turns were swallowed by the jungle surround-ing them.

Trees shielded the pond from most of the sunlight. Grass and vines clung to the rock face on either side of the waterfall itself, and the surface of the pond below frothed with the power of the surging water slamming into it.

He smiled at the expression on her face, then turned and led the way along the rocks until they reached the pond.

"This is so beautiful," she said, looking up at him. "Thank you for bringing me here."

His smile faded slowly as he looked at her. "I wanted to see it with you. It's too far out from the hotels and the village for many of the tourists to know about. And most of the locals don't come here." He turned his gaze on the waterfall and the surrounding beauty before looking back at her. "So it's where I come when I want to be alone with my thoughts."

And he'd brought her here. Shared this with her. Her heart was touched and broken all at once. Who would he share his secrets with when she was gone? How would she bear it, knowing that one day he'd leave her memory behind and move on for good with some other woman?

"Teresa?" His brow furrowed and he set both hands at her waist. "Are you all right?"

No. "Yes. I'm fine." She nodded, plastering a smile she didn't feel on her face. "I should have brought a bathing suit."

His eyes flashed and his lips curved in a wicked, completely tempting smile. "Here you won't need one."

A swirl of excitement fluttered to life in the pit of her belly and she went with it. As Rico undressed, so did she, and in a few short seconds, they were jumping into the pool at the base of the waterfall, swimming toward the curtain of water dropping from the overhang.

She hooked her arms around Rico's neck and pressed close to him, loving the feel of his skin against hers. The cold, clear water fell over and around them, sealing them into a bubble of privacy that seemed to lock the rest of the world away. Here it was only the two of them. And that was just as she wanted it.

When he kissed her, Teresa gave him everything she

had, everything she was. She poured her heart into the kiss and hoped he could feel her love in her touch.

His hand dropped to her core and slowly rubbed her center until she was writhing in his arms. The cold water on her skin and the heat he engendered with his touch combined to make Teresa feel as if she were about to splinter. And when her climax hit, she clung to him, their mouths fused, their breath sliding from one to the other and just for that perfect moment, they were *one*.

Much later, after making love in a patch of sun-warmed grass, the two of them lay sprawled together beside the waterfall. The roar of the water was the only sound and Teresa was torn between sheer happiness and the grief of knowing that all too soon this time with her husband would end.

"What will you do when the month is up?"

She tipped her head back to look up at him. "I don't know. Go back to my apartment in Naples, I suppose."

Features grim, he nodded and said, "I've been thinking about this, as well, Teresa."

"Really?" Was he going to ask her to stay? Could he put aside what had happened between them five years ago and allow for a future? Hope, that treacherous little beast, jumped up and down inside her.

"Yes." He went up on one elbow and looked down at her. All trace of the romantic was gone from his expression. His features were drawn and tight and the hope inside her withered a bit in response.

This couldn't be good.

"I've been thinking that you should not leave the island."

And just like that, hope was back. She smiled up at

him and felt the strangling knots around her heart loosen a little for the first time in years.

"You want me to stay?" *Please say yes.*

"Yes," he said. "At least until we know if you are pregnant."

This was why she rarely allowed hope to inflate inside her like an oversize balloon. Because when the inevitable happened and that balloon popped, the fall back to reality was a crushing one.

Rico didn't want her. He wanted the child they might have made together. So much for fresh chances. For starting over. He couldn't let go of the past and she couldn't change it for him, so they were at a standstill.

"That's why you want me here," she said, for her own benefit more than his. She needed to hear herself say it. "Because I might be pregnant."

"You will admit, there is a good chance you are." He laid one hand against her flat abdomen as if already claiming the child that *might* be inside her. "And if you are, you will stay here. With me. No divorce."

She pushed away from him and scrambled to her feet. Looking down on the gorgeous man sprawled naked in the sunshine, she felt only disappointment. Regret. And a deep, bone-searing sorrow that would probably be with her for the rest of her life.

"But the only way you want me is if I'm pregnant." God, it cost her to say those words.

"I did not say that," he countered, coming to his feet in a slow, languid movement.

"You really didn't have to," she muttered, pushing her still-damp hair back from her face with both hands. "God, I'm an idiot."

"Teresa? Surely you see that we are good together. Staying married wouldn't be a hardship on either of us."

His tone was so reasonable. The look on his face so patient. Teresa wanted to scream.

Shaking her head, she reached for her clothes and tugged them on while she talked. "No, Rico. I won't be part of a marriage that's described as *not a hardship*."

"You are deliberately misconstruing what I said."

"I don't think so," she countered, shooting him a quick glare while she hopped on one foot to pull on her shorts. "I think you said just what you meant."

He got dressed too, but with more casual, easy movements than she managed. "You are overreacting."

"Really?" She hooked her bra and then grabbed her shirt. Pulling it on, too, she asked, "Then what would your reaction be if I asked you to forget about prosecuting my family?"

He went still as stone, his pale blue eyes fixed on her, looking like chips of ice.

"Could you let them go?" She already knew the answer but she had to hear him say it.

Then he surprised her. Again.

"If I let them go," he said shortly, his voice as cool as the gleam in his eyes, "what do I get out of it?"

She threw her hair back out of her eyes. "I'll stay with you."

"For how long?"

This cost her. Humiliation flushed her cheeks as she realized she was blackmailing her husband into keeping their marriage alive. He wanted her. The passion between them was strong. And this last week she'd seen a side of him she hadn't seen since five years before. Maybe, she told herself, if she stayed and they were together long enough, love would eventually win the day.

"Forever," she said simply, surrendering her last ounce of pride. "Or for as long as you want me."

He took a long, deep breath and steadied himself. His eyes were shuttered, emotions sheathed to keep her from reading whatever he was thinking. It seemed to take forever before he finally said, "It's a deal. The Corettis go free and you stay here. With me."

She should have been happy. This was exactly what she had wanted so badly. To be able to remain with Rico here on the island. But getting it this way left her feeling as empty as she had during the previous five years. She could only nurture that small, now silent surge of hope and pray that eventually it would prove enough to conquer Rico's heart at last.

That hadn't gone at all as he'd planned.

Rico had spent the last week being the most attentive husband in the world in an attempt to get her to beg him to let her stay. That way he could keep his word to her family and hold on to his pride at the same time.

But she'd turned the tables on him.

Pacing the perimeter of his office two days after their sojourn at the waterfall, he felt caged. As if somehow he had wandered into a trap of his own making and now there was no way out.

"It was telling her that I wouldn't let her leave if she was pregnant," he muttered, scraping one hand across the back of his neck.

But he didn't know how he could have handled that any differently. Yes, he wanted her. Yes, he *loved* her still. But he couldn't tell her that without handing her all of the power in the negotiation that was sure to follow. So instead he got a wife who had once again become a hostage for her family.

She had traded her freedom for theirs and now he would never know if she would have chosen to stay simply because she loved him.

"Idiot." He kicked his desk for good measure as he made another pass around the room and the resulting pain was only what he deserved.

When his secretary buzzed through, he answered angrily, "I don't wish to be disturbed."

"I know, sir, but there's a man here to see you. He says it's urgent."

Scowling, Rico demanded, "Who is he?"

"He says his name is Gianni Coretti and that you're expecting him."

Twelve

Rico felt a surge of both anger and satisfaction. At last there was a target for the fury writhing inside him. "Send him in."

Gianni Coretti was tall, with short black hair, sharp brown eyes and the look of a man who didn't have much patience. Good, Rico thought. Then they were well matched. Gianni was wearing a well-cut suit and looked more like the head of a corporation than an infamous thief.

He crossed the room in several long strides and offered his hand. Rico merely looked from the outstretched hand and back up to the man's eyes. He gave nothing away, though mentally he was shouting, *Why are you early? I still have four days with Teresa!*

Which was ridiculous, of course. The whole point of this bargain he'd begun what felt like a lifetime ago was to have the Aztec dagger returned. That piece of family history that had been entrusted to him by his father. That's what he should be interested in. Instead all he could think was, if Gianni was here with the dagger, then Teresa would go.

But no, a voice in his mind whispered. She wouldn't. She'd bargained herself away for his assurance that he wouldn't see the Corettis jailed. Teresa was going to stay.

For all the wrong reasons.

Damn it.

"I've heard quite a bit about you from my father and brother," Gianni was saying as he let his hand drop to his side.

One eyebrow lifted. "Not flattering, I imagine."

"Not in the slightest," Gianni agreed with a grin. "But that's not important now, is it? I have what you asked for." He reached into his suit jacket and from the inner pocket pulled a cloth-wrapped item. "You can have it as soon as I have the evidence you gathered against my family."

Rico only crossed his arms over his chest and braced his feet wide apart. "Let me see the dagger first."

Gianni chuckled and shook his head. "This is what is wrong with the world today. No one trusts anymore."

Amused, Rico pointed out, "Says the thief."

"Touché, and yet it saddens me that the world has become such a cynical place."

He hadn't expected to almost like Teresa's brother, but damned if he didn't. "Makes stealing more difficult, does it?"

"There is that," Gianni acknowledged as he carefully unwrapped the ancient dagger he'd stolen five years before. "This…is magnificent." His gaze locked on the antiquity, he smiled as if watching a lover. "Intricate carvings, jewel-encrusted handle—but it's the *history* behind this piece that sings to me." He glanced at Rico. "And to you, I believe."

"Yes," Rico admitted, barely glancing at the once all important dagger. "It has been in my family for generations and we have all, at one time or another, felt the hum of history in that blade."

Gianni nodded, still studying the dagger. "When I took this from you, all I saw was its beauty. The jewels, the gold." He shrugged. "I am a mercenary man, trained to appreciate the finer things."

"That belong to others."

"As you say." Gianni shrugged that off and continued while Rico listened, oddly fascinated. This should have been a short meeting. An exchange and then a fast goodbye. Instead, Teresa's brother was acting as though they were old friends settling down for a visit.

"As I was saying," Gianni mused, looking down at the dagger in his hand, "when I first took the dagger, all I saw was its worth. But I couldn't bring myself to fence it. Couldn't sell it. It became a part of my collection and also, it became a sort of talisman."

"What do you mean?" Interested in spite of himself, Rico waited for an answer.

"As I held this dagger in my hands, for the first time in my life I felt the history of a piece." He turned it, studying it thoughtfully. "And I began to see that I had not been taking *things* from people. I had been stealing away pieces of their lives."

Surprised, Rico only stared at him. This was not the kind of thing he expected to hear from a professional thief.

"I, too, was shocked by this revelation," Gianni admitted with a wry smile. "It is not the sort of feeling a thief most appreciates."

"I don't think your father and brother share your philosophy."

"No." Gianni laughed and shook his head. "Not yet, anyway. But everything changes, does it not?"

He'd said that to Teresa not so long ago, Rico realized. And now all he could think was that *some* things would never change. He would always love her. And because he did, he realized what he had to do.

He had to let her go.

Rico had always thought that cloying cliché, "if you love something, set it free," was bull. He believed more in the "if you love something, hold on to it with both hands so you don't lose it" way of thinking. But now he understood that cliché. It tore at him to realize the hard truth, but there was no other choice for him.

Teresa had once again given up her own life for the sake of her family. She had once again made a sacrifice. The last time, he hadn't been a part of it. He had been left out of her choice altogether. Thinking back, he couldn't say what he might have done had she come to him with the truth. Would he have seen past his own anger at her lies? She'd kept so much from him back then. But had he been any more honest? They had fallen in love so quickly and their marriage was so new they hadn't had time to build the bridges of trust that would have seen them through bad times.

So. Would he have had her family arrested five years ago? He didn't know. He only knew what he should do *now*.

"Your ultimatum," Gianni said quietly, "had my family scrambling all over Europe to find me."

Rico laughed shortly and brought his mind back to the conversation at hand. "Your father thinks you should answer your phone."

Gianni grinned. "If I did that, he would call me more often."

"I feel the same about my own family at times." A shame they were meeting as enemies, since Rico had the feeling the two of them might have been friends.

"Well, then, we two have some business to conduct," Gianni said, holding the dagger so that the overhead light caught the blade and glinted like diamonds. "Here is your property. And now I would like to see this evidence my father claims you hold."

Rico nodded, walked to his desk and unlocked the top drawer. He took out a thick manila envelope and carried it to Gianni. Handing it over, he said, "That is everything I collected over five years." As a compliment of sorts, he added, "There wasn't much to be found."

Gianni grinned. "The Corettis are not easy to catch."

"I noticed," Rico said and took the dagger when it was offered.

The heavy gold weight felt solid, right, in his hands. He was relieved to finally have it back and yet…it felt like a hollow victory. He had set his sights on the return of his property and hadn't looked beyond that. Now he could see that retrieving his dagger could cost him the woman he loved.

Gianni opened the envelope and flipped through a few of the pages. He whistled low and long before looking up at Rico. "What you have here would have seen me and my family locked away for some time." He tucked the pages back inside and slapped the envelope against his palm. "Tell me, would you really have done it? Seen Teresa's family jailed?"

Setting the dagger down onto his desk, Rico pushed one hand through his hair and looked at the other man, standing quietly, watching him. It was past time for complete honesty, he thought. With himself as well as everyone else.

"Had you asked me that question two weeks ago," he said, "the answer would have been yes. Absolutely. Now…"

Gianni's eyes warmed as he smiled. "You *do* love her. My sister."

"I do."

"Which makes what I have to say next that much more uncomfortable. You have to release her from this bargain you and she struck."

"I know."

Gianni's eyebrows lifted high on his forehead. "You surprise me. I'd thought I would have to…convince you to uphold your end of the bargain."

"The bargain has nothing to do with this. Letting her go is the right thing to do," Rico said, a sharp stab of pain accompanying those words.

The thought of losing her broke his heart. But if he kept her here, he would never really *have* her. If she left… there might be a chance for them later.

"My father was right about you," Gianni said softly. "You are a dangerous man."

Before he could figure out what the other man meant by that, his office door flew open and Teresa stormed inside. She was wearing her white chef's uniform and as she slammed the door behind her, she snatched the hat from her head and tossed it aside.

"Teresa," her brother said warmly, "you look won-derful."

"Gianni, I'm not leaving," she said flatly.

"How did you know he was here?" Rico asked.

"Your assistant called to tell me when Gianni arrived. I had a soufflé in the oven and couldn't get away until just now."

Rico sighed and shook his head. She had friends all over the hotel and they were apparently willing to spy for her.

"Your brother was just leaving. As are you," Rico said. "The bargain is finished. Go back to your family."

She looked as though he'd slapped her and he winced. It wasn't his intention to bring her more pain.

"We talked about this, Rico," she reminded him, hands at her hips. "I'm staying."

"I've reconsidered." He ignored Gianni just as Teresa was. "We made a deal. The month is over."

"You can't mean this," she muttered. "What if I'm pregnant?"

"Pregnant?" Gianni scowled at Rico.

He waved the man's outburst away with one negligent hand and focused solely on Teresa. "Are you?"

Teresa chewed on her bottom lip, then grumbled, "No."

Disappointment welled inside him as his last hope at keeping her faded. But he had to do this for her. Damn it, he had blackmailed her into a monthlong affair. He would not blackmail her into being his wife. Since reason wasn't working with her, he released the anger churn-ing inside him.

"You think I *want* you to be a sacrifice for your fam-ily? *Again?*" He shook his head. "No, Teresa. You'll go and you'll do whatever it is you want to do without worrying about trading your life for theirs."

"No one asked her to sacrifice—"

"Be quiet, Gianni," she snapped and took two furious steps closer to Rico.

He saw the fire in her golden eyes and loved her even more. She was magnificent in her fury as she was in every other aspect of her life. This woman was everything to him. And his only chance to prove that was to force her to go.

"I don't want you here," he blurted out.

She sucked in a gulp of air and fired another glare at him as she shook her head. "You're *lying,* Rico. You said you didn't lie to those you care about, but you're lying now."

"Teresa, I think we should—" Gianni said patiently.

"*Basta!* Enough!" She snapped the words out and held up her hand, palm out toward her brother. Gianni shrugged and leaned one hip against Rico's desk, settling in to watch the show.

"You're an idiot," she said, frowning at Rico.

Gianni laughed.

Rico scowled and murmured, "Thank you."

"I'm not *sacrificing* myself by staying here, Rico," she said, coming closer now, keeping her gaze fixed on his. "I'm staying because I *love* you."

A flare of heat swelled in his chest and Rico breathed easy for the first time since she had stormed into his office. Maybe there was light in his darkness after all. "I love you, too. I always have."

Tears swamped her eyes and a tremulous smile curved her mouth. Reaching up, she laid her hand on his cheek and sighed when he turned his head just far enough to plant a kiss in the center of her palm.

"What about before, Rico? The past. Will that always be there between us?"

That was one thing he was sure of. "I don't care about the past, Teresa. All that matters to me is the future. *Our* future."

"And my family?"

He slid a glance at Gianni, still watching them with a bemused expression on his face. "If I can handle the Kings, I think I can live with the Corettis." He pointed a finger at the other man. "As long as they stay out of my hotels."

"Agreed." Gianni nodded.

"But you were going to let me leave," Teresa complained, drawing his attention back to her. "Why?"

"Because you had to *want* to be here. With me. It had to be your choice," he whispered now, as if only the two of them existed. "But if you had left, I promise you I would have followed."

Her smile wobbled, then grew more bright. "Really?"

"I would have traipsed all over Europe and beyond, romancing you, seducing you, winning your heart until you chose to come home. With me."

"Home?"

"Our home. Here. On Tesoro."

"Our home, Rico, is anywhere we're together." She went up on her toes and kissed him lightly. "You are my family, Rico. And I will always choose you."

Gianni cleared his throat and stood up, interrupting. "I will tell Papa what happened here. He'll be disappointed that you're not coming home, but I think he'll understand."

Teresa went to her brother and hugged him tightly. "Thank you, Gianni."

He shrugged and kissed her forehead. "You should know," he said, talking to Rico now, "Papa will probably want another wedding for you two—since we weren't invited to the first one."

"Yes, about that," Teresa said.

"Doesn't matter now, little sister," he said, "as long as you're happy. And I can see that you are."

She grinned at him, then watched as he walked to the cold fireplace on the far wall. "Gas?" he asked.

"The switch on the wall," Rico told him, knowing just what the other man was going to do.

Gianni hit the switch, gas flames erupted and he went down on one knee in front of it. Carefully, he tossed the envelope of evidence onto the flames and watched as it burned. When it was nothing but curling paper and ash, he stood again to face his sister and Rico.

"Now that's done, I can go."

"Where, Gianni?"

"London, for now." He went to her and pulled her in close for another hug. Then, looking from her to Rico, he said, "You don't have to worry about me anymore. The reason Papa couldn't get me on the phone this month is that I've been in talks with Interpol."

"What?"

He smiled at Teresa's shock. "In exchange for immunity, I'm going to work with their people. Help them catch thieves for a change." He shrugged. "Could be fun. And I think I might be able to talk Paulo and Papa into doing the same."

"Good luck with that," Rico said on a laugh.

"It's worth a try," Teresa said and beamed at her brother. "I'm so proud of you, Gianni."

"Imagine. *Me*. Working for the police." Shaking his head, he walked to the door and paused only long enough to look back at Rico and say, "Treat her well, Rico. I'll be in touch."

When he was gone, Rico grabbed Teresa, pulled her against him and just held on. Burying his face in the curve of her neck, he inhaled her scent and dragged it so deep inside him he would never take another breath without tasting her on it.

"I love you, Teresa Coretti King."

"I'm going to want to hear that a lot," she said, leaning back to look up at him. "I love you so much, Rico. I always have. Living without you was so horrible—"

"Shh. That's done. It's gone. Neither of us will ever have to feel that misery again, that's all that matters."

"Being here. With you. On Tesoro. It's perfect." She leaned her head on his chest and whispered, "Take me home, Rico. To *our* home."

"First," he told her as he stepped away, "I have something for you."

"All I need is you, Rico."

He grinned at her. God, he felt freer than he had in years. Just hearing her say that filled him with the kind of joy he had never really expected to feel again. But this had to be done. "Trust me. This you need."

He walked to his desk, opened the top drawer and took out a small velvet box that he had looked at every day for the last five years. When he brought it to her, he opened it and Teresa gasped.

"It's your ring," he said unnecessarily. "The one you

left behind with your note, telling me only that you had to leave."

"Oh, God." She stared at the yellow diamond and clapped one hand over her mouth. "It almost killed me to take that ring off, Rico. It—you—meant everything to me." Shaking her head, she murmured, "You kept it. I can't believe you kept it all this time."

"Sometimes," he said, "I admit, I thought about selling it or even tossing it into the sea."

"Oh, God…"

"But something kept me from it," he admitted as he plucked the ring from the velvet and slid it onto her finger. He sealed it there with a kiss, then met her eyes, now drenched again in what he knew were tears of happiness. "I think a part of me knew that we would find our way to each other again.

"Because you are my one. My only. And now the ring—and you—are back where you belong."

"And this time," Teresa whispered as she lifted her face for his kiss, "my romantic, wonderful husband, it's forever."

"It is a deal," he said with a smile, then kissed her with all the love he held in his now healed heart.

* * * * *

#2275 FOR THE SAKE OF THEIR SON
The Alpha Brotherhood • Catherine Mann
They'd been the best of friends, but after one night of passion everything changed. A year later, Lucy Ann and Elliot have a baby, but is their child enough to make them a family?

#2276 BENEATH THE STETSON
Texas Cattleman's Club: The Missing Mogul
Janice Maynard
Rancher Gil Addison has few opportunities for romance, but he may have found a woman who can love him *and* his son. If only she wasn't investigating him and his club!

#2277 THE NANNY'S SECRET
Billionaires and Babies • Elizabeth Lane
Wyatt needs help when his teenager brings home a baby, but he never expects to fall for the nanny. Leigh seems almost too good to be true—until her startling revelation changes everything.

#2278 PREGNANT BY MORNING
Kat Cantrell
One magical night in Venice brings lost souls Matthew and Evangeline together. With their passionate affair inching dangerously toward something more, one positive pregnancy test threatens to drive them apart for good.

#2279 AT ODDS WITH THE HEIRESS
Las Vegas Nights • Cat Schield
Hotelier Scarlett may have inherited some dangerous secrets, but the true risk is to her heart when the man she loves to hate, security entrepreneur Logan, decides to make her safety his business.

#2280 PROJECT: RUNAWAY BRIDE
Project: Passion • Heidi Betts
Juliet can't say *I do*, so she runs out on her own wedding. But she can't hide for long when Reid, private investigator—and father of her unborn child—is on the case.

"**D**on't you ever get tired of acting?" Logan asked, his casual tone not matching the dangerous tension emanating from him.

"What do you mean?"

"The various roles you play to fool men into accepting whatever fantasy you want them to believe. One of these days someone is going to see past your flirtation to the truth," Logan warned, his voice a husky growl.

She arched her eyebrows. "Which is what?"

"That what you need isn't some tame lapdog."

"I don't?"

"No." Espresso eyes watched her with lazy confidence. "What you need is a man who will barge right past your defenses and drive you wild."

"Don't be ridiculous," she retorted, struggling to keep her eyes off his well-shaped lips and her mind from drifting into the daydream of being kissed silly by him.

"You can lie to yourself all you want," he said. "But don't bother lying to me."

It wasn't until he captured her fingers that she realized she'd flattened her palm against his rib cage. She tugged to free her hand, but he tightened his grip.

"Let me go."

"You started it."

She wasn't completely sure that was true. "What's gotten into you today?"

He smiled. "You know, I think this is the first time I've ever seen you lose your cool. I like it."

How had he turned the tables on her in such a short time?

"I'm really not interested in what you—"

She never had a chance to finish the thought. Before she guessed his intention, Logan lowered his lips to hers and cut off her denial. Slow and deliberate, his hot mouth moved across hers.

Scarlett wanted to cry out as she experienced the delicious pleasure of his broad chest crushing her breasts, but he'd stolen her breath. Then the sound of the doors opening reached them both at the same time. Logan broke the kiss. Eyes hard and unreadable, he scrutinized her face. Scarlett felt as exposed as if she'd stepped into her casino wearing only her underwear.

Breathless, she asked, "Did that feel like acting?"

Find out what happens next in
AT ODDS WITH THE HEIRESS
by Cat Schield

Available January 2014 from Harlequin® Desire.

HDEXP1213